THINGS TO DO
WHEN YOU'RE
GOTH IN THE
COUNTRY
&
OTHER
STORIES

THINGS TO DO WHEN YOU'RE GOTH IN THE COUNTRY & OTHER STORIES

CHAVISA WOODS

Seven Stories Press
NEW YORK • OAKLAND • LONDON

**Special thanks to Bekka Sartwell,
Steve Cannon, and Joseph Keckler.**

Copyright © 2017 by Chavisa Woods

Seven Stories Press
140 Watts Street
New York, NY 10013
www.sevenstories.com

Notes on previous publication:

"Things To Do When You're Goth in the Country." Published in the *Cobalt Review*, 2014. Winner of the 2014 Cobalt Fiction Prize.

"How to Stop Smoking in Nineteen Thousand Two Hundred and Eighty-Seven Seconds, Usama." Published in *Sensitive Skin Magazine*, 2013.

"A New Mohawk." Published in *Jadaliyya* magazine, 2012.

"What's Happening on the News?" Published in *Quaint Magazine*, 2016.

Library of Congress Cataloging-in-Publication Data

Names: Woods, Chavisa, author.
Title: Things to do when you're goth in the country / Chavisa Woods.
Description: New York ; Oakland : Seven Stories Press, 2017.
Identifiers: LCCN 2016043180 (print) | LCCN 2016050227 (ebook) | ISBN 9781609807450 (hardback) | ISBN 9781609807467 (E-book)
Subjects: | BISAC: FICTION / Literary. | FICTION / Short Stories (single author).
Classification: LCC PS3623.O6753 A6 2017 (print) | LCC PS3623.O6753 (ebook) | DDC 813/.6--dc23
LC record available at https://lccn.loc.gov/2016043180

Printed in the USA.

9 8 7 6 5 4 3 2 1

This book is dedicated to the memory of my grandfather, Douglas James (Jim) Woods, whose love was unparalleled.

CONTENTS

How to Stop Smoking in Nineteen Thousand Two
Hundred and Eighty-Seven Seconds, *Usama*
9

Zombie
47

Take the Way Home That Leads Back to Sullivan Street
89

What's Happening on the News?
119

A Little Aside
143

Λ New Mohawk
147

Revelations
175

Things to Do When You're Goth in the Country
209

HOW TO STOP SMOKING IN NINETEEN THOUSAND TWO HUNDRED AND EIGHTY-SEVEN SECONDS, *USAMA*

I asked no questions about anything. I just wanted to smoke cigarettes. Lots and lots of cigarettes.

I come back once a year to visit. I only stay a few days. I try not to ask too many questions. There's nothing I can do about the answers, anyway. I'm only here five days a year. I smoke a ton of cigarettes. I give some to my brothers. They can't always afford them. I can do that. I can almost always afford cigarettes and I can smoke cigarettes with my brothers.

I can also drink beer with them, and I can usually afford to buy them one dinner or one new outfit, depending on the mood of things.

This visit, I bought them dinner at a Mexican restaurant in a strip mall: El Rancherito. Even though it was in a strip mall across the street from the Super Walmart, and even though El Rancherito is to Spanish what Green Day is to punk rock (people who don't know better think it is), it was owned and run by real Mexicans, and the food was very good. The restaurant provided endless chips, which my brothers liked, as well as ninety-nine-cent beer pitchers, also a big plus. My little-little and I polished off these ninety-nine-cent pitchers with no help from my big-little.

I have two little brothers. My little little brother is smaller than my older little brother. He is my little little brother. My older little brother is big. He is my big little brother. It was six o'clock. We'd just finished the authentic Mexican strip-mall food and two ninety-nine-cent beer pitchers, and I was getting ready to head to the car and take them back to Big-little's place, when Big-little got a phone call from his cousin. My big little brother has a cousin who's neither related to me nor my little little brother. His cousin is somewhere in between their two sizes. Big-little's midsized cousin is only related to Big-little and not related to me or Little-little on account of us all three having different fathers. I don't know who is the father of this midsized not-cousin of mine, but he sure looked like a kid who could use a dad when I met him.

The phone call consisted of Big-little looking ponderous and saying "uh-huh" three times, after which he hung up and informed Little-little that he wasn't going back to his own place because this cousin of his was there. Big-little was going to get his average-sized girlfriend to come take him somewhere else for the night.

My little little brother had been planning on staying at my big little brother's place that night, since he had no place else to stay, so he said he was going to need to be dropped off there anyway, Not-cousin or no Not-cousin. Little-little's stuff was at Big-little's and he had nowhere else to stay. What could he do?

We stood on the sidewalk of the strip mall waiting for Big-little's girlfriend. I took out three cigarettes. We smoked them. I didn't ask any questions. It was raining. We smoked under the awning until Big-little's girlfriend pulled up. He got in her midsized car. Little-little and I finished our cigarettes. We got into the car I was driving. Little-little took off his shirt and tossed it in the backseat with his other shirt. We drove on to Big-little's house, where his, not our, cousin apparently was going to be, which made Big-little not want to be there, and I didn't know why, not that I had asked.

It was dark. Dark in the country is really very dark. The stars are bright. Big-little's house is not really a house, but a long, skinny trailer resting lopsided off a dirt road that comes off an old-route highway out on the edge of the woods. On the way there, Little-little told me that behind the trailer, through the woods, was a corn-field where this whacked-out kid is living in an abandoned shack, cooking meth. He knows this because he and his friend were riding bikes through the field the week before, and the kid came out and started shooting at them. Little-little said he could smell the meth chemicals cooking even from several yards away. He knows what it smells like because he used to cook meth years ago before he realized just how bad of an idea that was.

He was riding bikes out there because he goes around the woods and all the surrounding areas tearing apart abandoned houses for scrap metal he sells at junkyards. He makes between eighty and two hundred dollars a week this way, depending. But he hurts himself a lot. He was showing me a wound on his finger he had all wrapped up with duct tape from where he cut himself scrapping a few days before, as we pulled in alongside the muddy drive of the dark, now nearly invisible trailer. I flipped the key off. He flipped the interior car light on and displayed for me a long, jagged scar that ran along the inside of his forearm. This happened two months ago when a copper pipe he was prying out of a wall sprung the wrong way and tore him open from just above his wrist to the inside of his elbow. He showed me this scar with the emblematic wiry enthusiasm of my little-little, now twenty-four and still peachy keen, scrappy, scrapping his life away. When it happened, he told me proudly, he just stapled it together with superglue, then wrapped it tight with duct tape and kept on scrapping. He's a scrapper. The wound had done something that sort of resembled healing, so he figured it was all right. He turned the light off, rolled up a pair of shoes inside his two shirts, and asked if I wanted to come in for a second. I did want to come in. I wanted to smoke and I couldn't smoke in the car I was driving and it was raining outside.

We clopped up the wilting porch of the trailer where rotting furniture was rotting in the rain on the drooping, decaying wood. The porch was threatening to metamorphose into an organic life-form, or perhaps just mold itself back into the wet ground. Maybe the porch would liquefy and become a moat around the trailer and you'd have to float on the couch to get across. Maybe even, the couch would become an organic life-form and give you a guided speaking tour of the trailer moat as it floated you up to the door.

For months, my brothers had been telling me about these green floating gaseous orbs they see coming out of the woods that they think are coming from UFOs landing out there. But I think it's more of a combination of mold, the meth kid cooking out in the field, and also, last year the EPA cleaned off about fifteen miles' worth of toxic topsoil from this area. This was a prime county for asbestos factories in the seventies. The land is flat. It rains a lot. The toxic water seeps and sits. Oh well. Green, glowing orbs are a lot more fun to think of as alien life-forms than all that other crap, especially if you're living with them. Especially if there's nothing you can do about them. What are you going to do? *Try* and communicate.

Little-little opened the door. Inside, the trailer was pitch-black and smelled of mold. I stepped into the wet blackness. During the five-second count before the light was switched on, I noted that we were not alone in a painful way. In the not-so-distant darkness, I made out a small red light and someone breathing uncomfortably next to it. From the red light, sounds were coming out, static broken by broken voices announcing numbers and positions.

Little-little turned on a lamp. A few feet away, sitting next to the TV, was who I assumed to be Big-little's cousin. He was a doughy boy of about twenty-one, dressed in a stretched-out white T-shirt and blue jeans. His face was as white as his shirt and his eyes were swollen and glowed almost as red as the red light on the police scanner he held in his left hand. His right hand was holding on to the handle of a silver pistol, which he had pulled halfway out of his side pocket. "You guys scared the fuck out of me," he told us.

Little-little shook his head and hissed, then tossed his shirt-shoes bundle across the room like a Frisbee. "This is my sister," he said, pointing me out. I sat down on the damp couch, not the one on the porch, but the one inside the trailer, and lit a cigarette. I asked my midsized not-cousin if he wanted one. He didn't want one. He shoved the pistol all the way back into his pocket and went over to the window, peeking through the slitted plastic blinds out into the total darkness of the muddy road and surrounding woods. He kept flipping the blinds open and closed. They made a clinking sound like plastic change, worthless and desperate to accomplish some impossible purchase, his freedom.

"No one's out there," Little-little told him as he rummaged through a pile of clothing on the floor and tried out about five different shirts, a couple of T-shirts and two long johns, one green and brown camouflage patterned. I smoked my cigarette.

Not-cousin held the scanner up to his ear and listened to the sound of static and clicking. "It was you guys sitting out there with your lights on?" he asked, his red eyes dancing. I nodded and puffed. Little-little wanted a cigarette. I gave him a cigarette. He started smoking it. None of those shirts had worked, I guess. He was still shirtless. Those shirts were back on the floor, utter failures.

Little-little perched beside me on the arm of the damp couch, shirtless, barefooted and puffing. Not-cousin started pacing slowly. "Whatcha got?" Little-little asked him. He pulled the pistol out of his pocket and handed it over. Little-little flipped it around and made inspecting noises. The police scanner crackled. We all looked at it. Not-cousin waited and listened, then shook his head no. Little-little tossed the gun spinning in the air, then caught it three times. "I had one better than this just three weeks ago, a semiautomatic hand gun," he told me. "It was an amazing weapon, but I had to bury it. Put 'er down!" he boomed. I smoked. Not-cousin paced.

"You buried it," I said, trying to make it more of an affirmation than a question. Questions couldn't be a good thing. I've learned this over the years.

He handed the silver pistol back to Not-cousin. "Yeah, had to bury it back there."

"Ah, the gun's buried in the backyard here," I said, as a statement.

Not-cousin took his seat by the TV again. He was struggling very hard not to cry, so his face, instead of twitching or doing stuff people's faces do when they're upset, was unnaturally unmoving, pale around his red, dancing eyes. He watched us talk, his head tilted sideways, swallowing hard between every few breaths, cupping the police scanner like a sick bird in his left hand.

"Yep, had to bury it. No good now, I'll bet. Probably full of mud." My cigarette was done. There was no arguing with it. It was gone. I put it out in an ashy soda can on the coffee table. "Sucks too, 'cause it was expensive."

"Well, yeah, semiautomatic," I said as if knowingly.

Little-little hopped off the couch and began boxing the air. "When I bought it, I knew it was stolen, but I didn't know *how* stolen."

"*How* stolen," I repeated, not as a question.

"I guess it was evidence for some shit that went down up in Chicago, and that's why those dudes that sold it to me were getting rid of it," he told me as he KO'd the invisible man. Number two came up to fight.

Not-cousin finally did something besides look desperate. He let out a moan and said, "That was dumb of you to buy that. They almost got you for that. They knew you had it. Came up here looking for it. It's a good thing they didn't have a warrant."

Little-little let his head go yesing. Fuck it. I lit another cigarette. Little-little put his out. Not-cousin had his own hidden away, menthols. He took one out and started smoking it, his fleshy lips quivering all around the butt. "I gotta get out of here. They've been here too many times."

"It's hot here," Little-little agreed. "But they never found nothing, and now I got my legal gun card, anyway." He magically produced a tan, laminated card from his back pocket. He waved it around proudly between air-boxes, and low and behold, I saw the truth in the light. My scrappy, peachy keen little-little was now indeed the proud owner of a certified license stamped with approval by the very civilized government of the US of A and the great State of Illinois, attesting his god-given right to bear lethal firearms. Hallefallujah.

He shoved the card back in his pocket and hopped over to the other side of the room where a small hatchet lay next to the armchair. He picked up the hatchet and started hacking at the arm of the armchair. This obviously wasn't the first time he'd hacked at the arm of the armchair. It had some notches already hacked out of it. "Damn thing's falling apart," he hollered as a joke. "I picked up Uncle Tiny's ax the other day. I swear to god, sis, I just barely touched it. Damn thing fell apart. And that's what Tiny said, 'Put that down, boy,' as soon as I touched it, but it was already too late. He said that thing's been out there on that block for ten years, withstood wind and rain and storms, blood sweat and tears, I laid my little pinky on it and the wood handle crumbled right away." He took one last satisfying hack at the arm of the armchair, then dropped the hatchet to the floor. My second cigarette was nearing the end, but I was already thinking about the third. Little-little's eyes twinkled pain like a bad joke at me from across the room. "I guess I got the opposite of the golden touch. Everything I put my hands on crumbles to crap."

"Maybe if you didn't come at stuff with axes in your hand, it wouldn't do that," I said dryly. He grinned big at this and flopped into the lap of the armchair.

All this was making Not-cousin more nervous. I put out my second cigarette and tongued the infection I could already taste beginning to form in the back of my throat. My glands were rough, swollen, and had that metallic taste skin on the inside of your mouth gets when it's sore. It made me cringe. I decided to wait a few minutes before I lit up a third smoke. But I didn't know what to do in the time between. There was nothing in my hands. My mouth was empty. I had no reason to be there anymore. I started seriously wondering what Not-cousin was doing there with a police scanner and a gun. I mean, I knew he was hiding out from the police. But in the absence of smoking, I couldn't help but think about things like *why*. Before I knew it, a question was coming out of my mouth. "What are you charged with?"

You know that look very young boys get when they are being punished severely for something, and they think it's very unfair? You might see them, about nine years old, hiccuping on a playground, nose running, slobber all over, Wiffle bat at their feet, the teacher asking, "*Did* you hit Georgy with the bat?" Then they let out a too-loud, quivering, "*Yes!* I did it. But! But! But!"

Well, that's pretty much what happened when I asked this question. He finally let his face go quivering and his eyes teared up and he blurted out his answer in that high, desperately pinched voice that one would expect to hear a kid use when he was admitting to hitting Georgy with a Wiffle bat. But what he said was, "Manslaughter two," in that voice, so it all had a bit of a different feel than the playground scene.

"Mm-hmm. Second-degree manslaughter," I repeated, trying to get back to statements.

"It's a bunch of bullshit," Little-little hollered from the lap of the hacked-up armchair. "They can't prove anything. They don't got proof of those texts. You threw your phone away, didn't you?"

"Yep."

"Where?"

"In the pond back there." Not-cousin pointed behind himself. He was referring to the small pond on the edge of Big-little's property. I started adding things up in my head. At least we had one *very* stolen semiautomatic handgun wanted as evidence in connection with *"some shit that went down in Chicago"* buried in the backyard, and one cell phone wanted as evidence for a man-slaughter-two case sunk in the pond. The ground I was sitting on was fertile with evidence of crime. *Crime Garden,* I thought, and wondered what else one might be able to find beneath the toxic topsoil. I racked my brain for any incriminating paraphernalia I might have on my person, thinking this would be the best place ever to chuck it. I wanted to add something to the plot.

"They don't got shit," Little-little went on. "Sis, it's dumb. You got a cigarette?" I took one out. He held up his hands. I tossed it across the room. The cigarette flipped through the air like a slow-motion kung-fu ninja. Little-little leapt up with the spry of a cat and caught it, then sat back down in the lap of the hacked-up armchair. "Naw, they don't got nothing. Listen to this shit, sis, and you tell me if you think it's right." Little-little lit up. My pack was already out, so what the hell, I lit up another one, too.

"All right."

Little-little tilted his head back and blew smoke rings into the air. They hung around looking like flying saucers above him. "He was dating this girl for a while," Little-little told me, pointing at Not-cousin. "Then he met this other girl he liked better, and he started getting with her."

"I cheated on her," Not-cousin let out in a whimper, his neck already crooked for an execution.

"Right, but then he told his girlfriend the truth and broke up with her," Little-little continued. "She freaked out. She was only, like, seventeen, and she had problems anyway. Really, dude. She had problems."

Not-cousin's red eyes were sparkling in his doughy head. "I know," he cracked out in a whisper.

"Last week, his ex-girlfriend sent him all these text messages saying she was going to kill herself if he didn't come back to her. She said if he didn't come over right then, she was going to do it. And he didn't answer them or come back to her, and she killed herself."

"She killed herself," I said. "Wait a minute. You're saying she killed *herself?*"

"Hung herself," Little-little told me, acting out the noose-snapping motion with his hand in the air and his neck falling sideways.

"I never saw the texts before it happened," Not-cousin blurted out, his whole body becoming a pale, quivering mess. "I swear I didn't see them." The police scanner crackled. He twitched, then fidgeted with the dial. We all got quiet, listening. It was hard to make out what they were saying. It was mostly numbers. I guess he was listening for his name.

I was becoming even more confused. "What does it matter if you saw them or not? I don't understand." They didn't respond, but stared intently at the scanner. I kept on with my endless questions. "How are they charging you when they know she hung herself? They don't think you helped her hang herself, do they?" Now everything was a big question. Fuck. I sucked on my smoke.

Little-little jumped up and went to the window that looked over the backyard and the woods. "Shit, I think I see one. There it is. Come here." I got up and went to the window. I didn't see anything. "It was there for a second," Little-little told me.

I turned back to Not-cousin and repeated my question. "Do they think you helped her hang herself?"

Not-cousin was a young man who was trying too hard not to cry. He remained silent. Little-little spoke for him, keeping one eye out the window, watching for green, glowing alien orbs. "Sis, don't you get it? She hung herself because of him, and they're charging him with second-degree manslaughter." He sucked his cigarette and looked at me like I was stupid.

My cigarette was done, so I just lit up the next one on the end of that one. "That's not how manslaughter two works!" I said, my voice all jumpy, becoming exasperated.

Little-little let out a frustrated sigh. "There's some law in this county that says if you get a message like that, or a phone call, where someone is threatening to kill themselves or someone else, or bomb something or shit, that you got to report it or you're responsible. It's like, 'If you see something, say something,' you know?"

I rolled my eyes. "It's like a Good Samaritan law," I said. "Ah." Little-little shrugged, pinched his cigarette out between his finger and thumb, and went back to staring intently out the window. "Or maybe it's because of the Patriot Act?" Not-cousin turned the dial on the police scanner. "Either way, it's bullshit," I told him. "They can't get you for that. There's no way they have any legal ground to stand on. No one's going to want you to go to jail for that, because that would set this crazy precedent that would make everyone around here liable for every crazy fuck who threatened anything."

For a moment a glimmer of hope sprinted across Not-cousin's red eyes. I even saw a hint of a smile light on his lips. "Ya think so?" he asked just above a whisper. But then everything went shitty again. He looked to the ground and shook his head no, answering his own question. "It don't matter anyway. I broke my probation now, so they're coming to put me up either way."

"Probation. You were on probation?" He nodded. "For what?"

"Rape," Little-little answered for him.

"Oh. Rape." I put a period at the end of those words. I was still smoking my cigarette, but I wanted another one. I wanted ten another ones. I wanted to line up all the cigarettes I could fit between my lips like overgrown teeth and set them on fire.

"*Statutory*," Not-cousin added, chewing his cheek. "Damn, man, statutory. Always say *statutory* first, okay?"

"Whatever." Little-little gave up his disappeared-green-orb watch for a minute to go to the kitchen and get a glass of water. "That was dumb, too. You want a drink, sis?" The dishes in and around the sink were piled up an extra foot above cabinet level and looked like they hadn't been washed in years, literally. They could accompany the talking couch in giving guided tours across the trailer moat. Put some suspenders on those dishes, they could have passed for tour guides.

"Nah. I'm good," I replied.

"She was his girlfriend," Little-little told me from the kitchen. "She was sixteen, and he was nineteen. Her mom's a Christian and all, and she didn't like him. When she found out they'd been having sex, she called the cops on him."

"What's the age of consent in Illinois?"

"Seventeen."

"Well at least this girl who killed herself wasn't a statutory thing, too," I said. Not-cousin nodded. Little-little came back with his glass of water and sat down next to me. "Still, you can beat this." It felt weird telling him this, because I'm not the kind of lady who usually sides with convicted rapists wanted for manslaughter. "The longer you break your probation, the longer you have to serve," I went on. "Your best bet is to turn yourself in and fight this. Have some people write letters to the paper outlining your case. Hell, call the ACLU. They might provide a free lawyer or at least get you some publicity. There's no way people are going to support prosecution. People will think it's crazy. No one wants to be liable for what their ex or what someone else *threatens* to do. The DA won't touch it. No way."

They were both looking very confused at me. They were looking at me like I was a floating green alien gas orb. Not-cousin shivered as if shaking off my incomprehensible statements. "I been to jail once already. Seven *months* was too long." He swallowed hard and tensed his quivering jaw. "I ain't going back. It don't fuckin' matter. One way or another, I ain't going back."

"Don't you start talking like that! I swear to god, man. Don't you fucking talk like that!" Little-little was on his feet suddenly, shouting. "Give me the gun! Dude, give me the gun!" Not-cousin swatted him away as he reached for it.

I watched them argue over the gun, continuing on with my cigarette chain gang. I knew why he was reacting this way. I knew what "I'm not going to jail one way or another" meant, too. When Little-little was nineteen, he and some of his friends had a little meth lab set up for themselves, also out in the woods, but in a different woods. Four of them got busted. But not Little-little. He was lucky enough not to be around that day. That's all. His best friend, who was also nineteen, got slammed with some serious time, several years in prison. Instead of going to prison, though, that kid shot himself in the head.

Little-little still talks about him and how grateful he was for the short time he was blessed to have known him. He hasn't gone near the dragon since, no matter how broke he is.

I felt really dumb for everything I'd just said to them. What was I thinking? They kept arguing, like in a ballet in front of me. I tried to blow smoke rings, but failed. What a stupid little faggot

I was. I thought about what a stupid little faggot I was; about my stupid little art-fag clothes, and how I was talking at them with my faggoty, self-educated voice, telling them my faggoty New York ideas. I'm such a queer faggot, I was even thinking about Michel Foucault. I was thinking about how he said, *"The guilty person is only one of the targets of punishment. Punishment is directed, above all, at others, at all the potentially guilty."* I was thinking that, here and now, where I was, Michel couldn't have been *wronger*. There's always this faggoty debate about the three possible purposes of prisons being reform, punishment, and/or dissuasion. I started laughing thinking about it. What do academics know?

Little-little hasn't been off probation for more than a few months at a time since he was thirteen. Every time he breaks any part of his probation, whether it's a ticket, a missed phone call, or a failure to report a change in address, he goes to jail. Every time he goes back to jail, he accumulates more fines and goes in longer than the time before. He's in his early twenties, and pretty soon, they're going to get him. He has a snake wrapped around his ankle, its tail is tied to an anvil, and he's hanging off the edge of a cliff. He spent the last five years of his childhood being illegal. He's spent the majority of his adult life being illegal. He's an illegal person. He's been marked as such, and as soon as they can, they will remove him. They will find whatever trumped-up reason to remove him, and for as long as possible. They will remove him.

And people will be glad. People will not be dissuaded. People will be relieved. He will not be reformed *or* punished, simply removed.

Keep America Clean. Please use provided containers.

Sometimes things are extremely simple.

I could tell Not-cousin was the same kind of case. He generally just seemed illegal. They both did. You could look at them and tell. They were illegal people. Eventually they would be removed.

Little-little finally had possession of the gun and was walking it down the hallway that led to the bedroom. He was putting the gun to bed. The gun was real sleepy and had started fussing. But when he got it in there, it went down easy as cold, hard steel.

I tried another smoke ring. It failed. Not-cousin went back to flipping the switch on the police scanner. Finally, some words came out of me that didn't sound like stupid, gay New York words. "You need a plan. You got a plan?" He shrugged. Little-little came back in, then went through to the kitchen and searched around the fridge for a beer. "Maybe," I tried, "you should leave Lebanon. There are only three thousand people here. If you just drive for fifteen minutes, you'll be two towns away. They have different cops, cops who might not be looking for you so hard, cops who might not even know you."

"You think so?" he croaked out.

Not-cousin isn't the brightest bulb. "They just want to get rid of you," I told him. "If you can, leave the state. But at least, you have to leave the town. If you really don't want them to find you, at least get out of town."

Little-little went back to the window and sipped his beer. "Yeah, dude. They did find you here the last time."

"Ummmm," came out of my mouth like a long frog. *I should really leave soon, before the SWAT team bursts in,* I thought.

But it's hard to leave, sometimes. I knew that. This was the kind of place where people just stay, and stay, and stay. This place had staying power. The staying power had installed itself in Not-cousin's mind like an invisible electric shock line around a chicken coop. He hadn't received the shocks in quite a while, because he didn't even remember that it was an option to try and cross the line. It was not an option. If I hadn't been such a weird faggot, I might not have ever tried too hard, either. I was shoved repeatedly over the shock line at a young age. I was a chick that got shoved. At the time, it seemed like an awful happening, being ostracized for my strange plumage. Sitting there, though, I knew my feathers of faggotry were my privilege.

I shook my fancy feathers and extinguished a cigarette. Not-cousin's eyes met mine, glimmering. "Your brother said you live in New York. Is that true?"

I nodded. My feathers were too big. They were going to knock things over. They were going to put someone's eye out if I wasn't careful.

"New York *City*?"

"Yeah."

"Oh." Something was trying like hell to get out of his throat, but it was banging into something else down there, and making all kinds of weird noises. "How are you . . . well, I mean, how are you going back?"

Goddamnit. My fancy feathers drooped. My fancy feathers got all wet with shame and sorrow. My fancy feathers were impotent. They didn't really fly. They couldn't let me take anyone away. They just looked nice. I wanted to fold them up and hide them beneath my ridiculously sequined vest. "A plane. I'm sorry."

"Right, right," he nodded. "How much does that cost?"

I just shook my head no, solemnly. The words *A plane. I'm sorry* bounced around my skull like two clean sentences. Complete sentences. Heavy, cold, sculpted sentences. *A plane. I'm sorry.* Four words, two periods making up a real pair.

"It don't matter. It's a extradition state anyway," he told me, letting me off the hook.

"Fuck! Fuck! Fuck! Look, sis. There they are! Fuck! Quick, come here." Little-little was losing it by the window. Not-cousin and I both hopped up and took a place beside him. He pointed. "There they are. See them?" I didn't see anything. "Wait." Little-little flipped the light off. The three of us stood in the total darkness of the trailer listening to the mixed static of the police scanner, staring out the window. It was really very dark out there. The stars were trying to peek out through the mist left over from the rain. One could vaguely make out the silhouette of the forest line. "See? Right there," Little-little pressed. I scanned the trees' edges. As my eyes adjusted to the darkness, something became startlingly clear. Little-little might be crazy, but he wasn't bat-shit crazy, or we all were.

There, bouncing along the forest's edge, radiant as extracted souls, were two glowing green balls of gaseous light. But they didn't move like gas. They were balls that bounced, as if moving of their own internal agency. They bounced up and down like gummy bears. They bounced into and off of each other. They bounced back and forth and around and around like a children's song. They did all of this very slowly and unself-consciously, as if they were absolutely real and would have been surprised if you told them that their existence was a serious problem for humanity, for logic, science, and all that.

They bounced around for a good minute and a half, then they bounced back into the forest, totally out of sight. "What'd I tell ya? What'd I tell ya? That's what we saw the other day, isn't it?"

"Yep." Not-cousin nodded yes.

Little-little turned the light back on. "Hot damn, sis! You saw 'em?"

I nodded yes.

"Come on." He started going through the pile of shirts again. "Let's go out there and find 'em."

"Ummmmmmmmmm." Another long frog. "Yeah. I gotta get going." I picked up my bag, threw it over my shoulder, and headed to the door. Little-little followed skipping behind me.

"You can't go. Not after what you just saw," he said insistently.

"Yeahhhh. I gotta get going." I nodded and made an unfortunate face. "I'll call you tomorrow." He was totally stunned. But what could I do? I wasn't going out into the crime garden to hunt semi-intelligent glowing green orbs, with the possibility of a SWAT team breaking in any minute hanging over my head. I could deal with one thing or the other. Not both. Something in me had absolutely shut down. I wasn't cut out for that. That just wasn't my idea of a good night. I was supposed to meet an old high school friend at a bar at ten, anyway. I searched for some way to make things normal, to make things right. "Here. Take this. Keep it." I reached into my bag, retrieved an unopened pack of cigarettes and pressed it, like a talisman, into Little-little's hand. "Call you tomorrow," I told him. "Good luck," I told Not-cousin. "Be careful," I told them both.

I sped down the pitch-dark winding country roads. These roads were burned into my head like a map of crisscrossing scars. My mind was racing over several thoughts. I was thinking about how I probably look rich to my brother. I was thinking how broke I was in Brooklyn. I was thinking that if I changed my plane ticket and stayed a few months, I could probably help keep Not-cousin out of serving outrageous amounts of jail time for an outrageous charge. I was thinking, even if I was pretty broke, I had language, and they didn't. I was thinking about Pygmalion. I was thinking this would be madness on my part to stay and try to help him, because eventually, they both would do something else to land themselves in the slammer no matter how many marbles I shoved into their mouths, no matter how many times they repeated *"The rain in Spain,"* I moved away for a reason, I reminded myself. This place kills people, I reminded myself.

I slowed at an unlit railroad track and remembered that those same tracks had taken two of my uncles. One of them was a suicide. He just laid his head down there on the cold steel one night and let the train take care of the rest. The other uncle was working on the tracks and fell over from a heart attack and hit his head on a spike. He was a few months away from retirement, but was already too old for that kind of work. I was thinking about how much sad death, murder, and suicide I had seen there in the southern border of the rural Midwest, and how little I had seen since moving to a big city. I was thinking how ironic that seemed. But amid all these thoughts was one glaring thought that kept screaming at me that I was trying not to pay attention to. *What the fucking hell were those green glowing orbs that bounced around like gummy bears, seeming to move of their own agency?* This was not a good thought for driving down an empty country road at night. I flipped the doors to lock and turned on the radio, then pressed the pedal to sixty.

It took a moment for the news to register. It was repeating for a while before I really heard it. I was turning onto the lit road of an actual town, and could see my destination, "Chubby's Bar, Serving Spirits for More Than Forty Years," just beyond the stop sign, when the news knocked five times, hard on the cognizant part of my brain, and I let it step inside.

Hello, nice to meet you, "Osama bin Laden Is Dead." Come in.
Have a seat. Or not. Shuffle around awhile. You seem a bit unsettled.
I pulled into Chubby's parking lot and turned off the car, along
with the repeating news.

The bar was permanently stuck in the late seventies, in the best
way. Everything was black leather and red paint. A mirror made up
the wall behind the bar, reflecting bottles of spirits. Smoke hung
in the air, although it's no longer legal to smoke inside in Illinois.
Chubby's owner was a real rebel. The three people sitting inside
hushed and turned as I entered. They stared at me blankly. Not
quite like I was a green gaseous alien orb, but as if watching to see
if I might turn into one. I guess they weren't used to seeing chicks
in ties and vests with psychobilly faux-hawks around there. Weird
little faggot, I was. The staring lasted and lasted, even as I perched
myself on a barstool and tried to act casual, just a person wanting
a drink in a bar, the staring went on. "Can I get a whiskey, neat,
with a seltzer backer?"

The female bartender, who was now standing in front of me,
stared even harder. "Huh? What did you say?"

"A whiskey with nothing in it and a soda water, a seltzer, separate," I tried again.

"You just want me to pour you whiskey in a cup?" she said
angrily.

"Just like if you would do it on the rocks, but without the ice,"
I said timidly, almost as a question. This wasn't helping at all. I
thought it was the simplest thing I could have ordered. Apparently, it was an alien libation. An old man in a ball cap and overalls
nursed a Budweiser in the far corner. At a table near him, an old
woman sat twirling a straw in a Coca-Cola can with what appeared

to be the Bible open beside it. They were both still staring at me too. "However you usually do it is fine," I kept on.

"I don't never do nothing like any of that. You want *soda* (pause) *water*? You want that alone in a different glass? I don't have any of that. I might have some tonic in the back. You want that?"

I didn't give a shit about any of this. I just wanted to know if Osama bin Laden was really dead. But I had totally pissed off this bartender, and I didn't know how to un-piss her off. She looked like everybody's aunt. She was in her late thirties with clean, short blond hair, and generally appeared to be a legal, sane, normal person. But boy had my drink selection pissed her off.

"It's fine. I'll just take a whiskey and a regular water." She filled up a glass of water and set it in front of me, clankingly. Then she got a pint glass and headed for the whiskey. "Oh that's, yeah. Um. That's too big. I mean," I tried to make it a joke, "I can't hold my liquor that good. Ha! Not that I'm a drunk, but . . ."

She was now still, holding the whiskey and pint glass, glaring at me. "How big a cup *do* you want?" I pointed to a regular tumbler. If it is possible to point with embarrassment, that's what I did. She grabbed the tumbler and slammed it down in front of me. "Why don't you just tell me when." She started pouring. I told her when. She stopped. I got out my wallet. She stepped back and chewed her bottom lip, staring at the glass, then shook her head. "I don't know how much to charge for that," she said aggressively, as if asking me for an answer. I heard the old man "hmph" loudly in my direction. Then, thank god, the door opened behind me, and my old buddy from my teenage years, Jessica, stepped in.

"Hey there," she squealed, smiling the bright, perpetual smile of the kind of optimistic lady who can bounce into any bar in the southern rural Midwest without everyone turning to stare at her.

She hugged me and sat her pleasantly plump self down next to me. "Hey there. How you doing?" she asked the bartender.

"Just fine. What can I get you to drink?" the bartender asked, still suspicious, but seeming to thaw.

"I'll have a Hot Cherry Bomb, if it's not too much trouble," Jessica chirped.

"Coming right up," the bartender chirped back, very happy about knowing what someone meant again. She then proceeded to mix cayenne pepper, lime juice, Dr Pepper, vodka, and Red Bull in a pint glass, topping off the concoction with two cherries and a straw. Easy as pie. Hot Cherry Bomb. Sure. Why not? "That'll be four dollars."

Really? I thought. *Are these people fucking with me?*

The bartender eyed my drink, a little friendlier now. It was like magic. I had a translator. "I guess yours'll be three-fifty. That sound fair?"

"Fine by me." I laid my money on the bar and took out my cigarettes. "You can smoke in here," I told Jessica. She smiled and nodded. I lit up and sipped my whiskey. I wasn't being stared down anymore and could finally pay attention to something besides my drink order. The television above the bar showed what appeared to be hundreds of frat boys waving American flags. The bartender noticed me watching.

"They got him. Can you believe it?"

"I just heard. Just before I came in."

"Where've you been?" Jessica asked. "It happened hours ago."

"I'll turn it up." The bartender went to the TV and turned the volume on. The news anchors just kept repeating, "Osama bin Laden is dead," in slightly different ways each time. Sometimes they said, "Osama bin Laden has been taken out." Sometimes they said, "Osama bin Laden was successfully killed by SEAL Team

Six," and sometimes they said, "Barack Obama is dead, I'm sorry I mean . . . Osama . . ." It was Fox News they were watching. Everyone in the bar was staring intently at the screen, but no one seemed very happy about it. They looked much happier in New York City, where the world's largest and most morbid tailgate party had suddenly erupted at Ground Zero. I read the words scrolling across the bottom of the screen: "Usama bin Laden Is Dead."

I hmphed. "Jesus, they can't even spell it right."

Bin Laden's face popped up like a Hungry Hungry Hippo. Then the thin, wrinkled old lady with the Coke popped up like a Hungry Hungry Hippo as well, right up off her barstool, and growled, "Yer dead now, motherfucker. We gotcha, motherfuckerrrrrr!"

"Calm down, Iris." The bartender smacked the bar counter. Iris went back into the pond.

"I really like this place," Jessica chirped. "It's weird." She smiled big and giggled. "I'll have to come back again sometime." She looked around herself. "It's like another world in here." Jessica grew up two towns away in a slightly bigger town. Chubby's was my hometown bar.

"Barack Obama has successfully killed Usama bin Laden," the news anchor said.

"*Obama* didn't kill him," the old man at the bar muttered at no one and everyone, "the *SEALs* killed him." He looked disgusted, like he'd just vomited a bit in his mouth. "*Obama,*" he sneered. "Hmph."

"I'm glad he's dead, anyway. We can all rest a little easier now," the bartender told us.

"What's your name?" Jessica asked sweetly.

"Donna."

Jessica introduced herself and me to Donna the bartender. "Where are you from?" Donna asked.

"She lives in New York City," Jessica told her proudly. I guess that question was mostly directed at me.

"New York City? Well then, you must be more excited about this than anyone," Donna told me.

I kept watching the TV. "They're spelling it wrong," I repeated. "Look."

Donna turned and looked. "Well, how 'bout that? They're spelling Osama with a *U*. Is that an alternate way or something?"

"I don't think so."

"Usama bin Laden is dead," the news anchor repeated. And I couldn't help but notice, she was pronouncing it by the new spelling. I extinguished my cigarette in the black ashtray.

"I don't think it's a mistake," I told them. Jessica smiled big at me. "It's on purpose, see, it's USA-m-a. They're doing it on purpose. They're renaming him as if he's now property of the USA. Get it? USAma."

"I'm not really a political person," Jessica said, shrugging and smiling. But Donna was listening and looking incredulously at the screen.

"That *is* weird," she concurred.

"I haven't seen you in years. Tell me everything," Jessica said, changing the subject.

"I've had about enough of that myself." Donna muted the TV and headed over to the jukebox. In a minute, Travis Tritt was serenading us.

"Tell me all about New York City," Jessica smiled big and her perfect eye makeup sparkled. "I want to know everything. I want to live vicariously through you." She leaned toward me excitedly. Her elbow bumped a cup that was sitting next to the ashtray. It fell over, spilling out a wad of cash and some change. I thought it was a tip jar, but as I put it back in its original position, I read the words scrawled on the side in black marker: "Donations for Chastity's funeral."

Jessica and I stared at it. Her smile fell down so hard it scraped its knees and looked like it might not be skipping around again for a while. I grimaced. "Oh. That's depressing." I slid the donation jar far away, out of sight and mind. I lit up another cigarette. When I exhaled, a noise came from my chest that sounded like Satan's dog with a throat infection. I started coughing.

Jessica recoiled. "That sounds *really* bad. Are you okay?" I banged on my chest with my fist. It felt like I had an alien in there. And I didn't have Sigourney Weaver around to come help me if it decided to burst through my chest. I gasped for breath, hunched over, and grabbed Jessica's wrist. She jumped.

"Listen, Jessie, forget about New York City. I don't even remember New York City. There's something weird happening around here," I whispered, and took up my desperate coughing again.

Jessica stiffened. I held tighter. "What do you mean?" she asked, her voice shaking with confusion.

"I saw these . . . *things*. These green things. I was out in the woods tonight, with this kid who's wanted for manslaughter," I whispered. Jessica's eyes got big and her eyebrows got all twisty. "It's only second degree. It's nothing. Forget it. Like I was saying, I saw these things . . ." Jessica was looking at me like I was crazy. I tried to figure out how to proceed. Someone touched my shoulder, softly tapping.

I turned to find Iris staring at me, nearly nose to nose. The wrinkles around her eyes looked like a dried-up beach. "Can we help you?" Jessica asked, trying to keep it cool.

Iris's thin lips moved. "The time is coming."

"I'm sorry?" Jessica came back. I let go of her wrist and swiveled around on my stool. My chest growled. Iris took a pamphlet out of her Bible and handed it to me. On the front was a picture of the sky and what seemed to be silhouettes of people floating up into the clouds. There were words printed in a very kitschy font across the blue sky: But what if it IS true?

"Iris! I told ya." Donna was coming out of the ladies' room. "I told ya, Iris," she hollered. "You can sit in here, but you gotta leave people alone."

"It's coming!" Iris informed us, nodding vehemently and side-stepping toward the door as Donna made her way toward her. "The time is coming. Prepare yourself."

"You gotta get now," Donna said, taking her by the arm. They walked out together.

I gasped and something in me growled louder. "Weird shit has been happening all night. I'm telling you. There's something going on." My level of paranoid desperation startled even me. I began to worry I might be losing my mind.

Jessica patted me on the shoulder and shook her head. "Calm down, hon. She's just a crazy old woman. Every bar has one."

She picked up my cigarette from the ashtray and started to put it out, but I snatched it from her and nearly shouted, "I'm not done smoking that!" The beast in me growled too. It was an unearthly double-growl. Jessica laid her hands squarely on the table and stiffened defensively, eyeing me from the side.

Donna came back in. "Sorry about that, girls. She does that all the time."

"It's fine," Jessica assured her, trying to get her smile back up off the sidewalk, but it was all wobbly. Donna went and sat at a booth far away from us and read the paper. The old man in the ball cap was still there at the other end of the bar, smoking and drinking, occasionally muttering at the screen. Silently, ten hundred million frat boys waved American flags, their bulbous lips chanting "U! S! A!" like a birth cry, as they held their glittering girlfriends up on their broad, white shoulders, above the streaming words "Usama bin Laden Is Dead."

"I hear you've been doing really good in New York. You just had a book published. How's that going?" She was trying so hard, poor thing.

The beast and me sucked down my cigarette loudly. "Yeah. I had a book published. It's going great. I got an award. Listen, Jessie, have you ever seen any, like, green orbs in the woods around here?"

Her face did a little dance. I realized, as I watched her face go from the twist to the two-step, that she was scared of me. She hadn't seen me in three years. How was she to know I wasn't totally bonkers? Luckily, she'd known me as a kid, so she was also concerned for me. She inhaled deeply and straightened herself. "Okay." That word was like a reset button. "You saw something you can't explain? Okay." Still resetting.

I nodded. "Yeah. I definitely saw something. Have you heard of anyone seeing, I know it sounds weird, but green floating balls?"

She pointed to my box of Winstons. "Can I have one?" I nodded and handed her a cigarette. "People have said they've seen things around here." She put the cigarette to her lips. I lit it. She sucked on it lightly, then picked up her drink and took a big sip from the straw. That thing could have been a chocolate milkshake the way she drank it right then. "I've only heard about silver saucers. Not green balls. Who knows. I've never seen anything like that. But I hear a lot of things. Farmers have always seen things. You know that." She shrugged. "We made fun of them. *You* made fun of them. I think they're a little crazy. Maybe it's sunstroke. But, I don't know." She stared up at the light, pondering. The alien beast in my chest gnawed at the end of my cigarette. "I did used to see this dead Indian in the field behind my house when I was little. My dad saw him a few times too. I've told you about that. You remember? The Indian ghost?"

I nodded. "That's right. I remember those stories. I thought you might just be trying to scare us, though. It was real?"

She set her drink down. "I think so. I know what I saw." We silently contemplated the existence of other worlds. "It's hard to tell, though." Her hand shook slightly as she ashed her cigarette. "Some things are a little fuzzy since the electroshock therapy."

"The what?"

"Oh I didn't tell you about that?" Her blond hair was perfectly cut in a bob. Her makeup was clean and shining. Her mouth always held a slight smile, even as she said those awful words. "It was nothing," she said, shrugging it off. "I just had a bad few months a couple of years ago. They did the electroshock therapy, and it really helped. It's just that now, some of my memories are a little fuzzy." I was looking worriedly at her now. Where the hell was I? What alternate universe had I fallen into? Apparently, you *can* go home again, but maybe you just *shouldn't*. "No it's fine," she told me reassuringly. "I got my degree. I have a great job, a nice house, a new boyfriend. I'm really happy."

She did look fine. She looked better than me. It all sounded just great except for the electroshock therapy part. "I didn't even know they still did that," I said.

"Sometimes they do," she chirped, and smiled, lifting her glass to toast. Toast what? I had no idea. But I toasted back.

The old man at the end of the bar muttered something and

raised his beer bottle. Donna came over to get him another. She asked me if I wanted another one of the same. I told her I did. She poured it easy as pie.

"Fuck the country, and fuck this country too," I said, lifting my glass for my own toast. Donna was already at the other end of the bar getting that old man beer, but I didn't give a damn if she could hear me. Jessica shuddered though. She didn't toast back. "Sorry, it's just been a really intense night. I'm an asshole." Her drink was almost gone and she wasn't ordering another. She had a look on her face like she wanted to leave.

"It's okay. I know you always hated it here." She patted my hand. "What the hell happened tonight? Did you say something about manslaughter?"

I shook my head no. "Yeah. It doesn't make any sense. This kid is hiding out from the police. He's wanted for second-degree manslaughter. He's staying at my brother's place. My big little brother. He's my brother's cousin. He's not my cousin. He's my not-cousin." I laughed out loud.

"You know what, I'll have another one too." She held up her glass. She was intrigued. Donna came over and started mixing the weird concoction. "What did you mean it doesn't make any sense?"

I gulped down the top third of my new whiskey and lit up another smoke. I like to smoke when I tell stories. "I don't see how anyone could call it manslaughter, of any degree. He had this girl-friend, and he cheated on her, broke up with her, whatever. She was, like, seventeen. She started sending him messages saying that if he didn't come over, she was going to kill herself. And he didn't and she—" The story was broken off by the sound of glass breaking on the old cracked floor, like a broken heart breaking over something that was already broken long before.

Donna's hands were cupped in midair like they were still holding cups and mixers, but they weren't. Her face was as pale as yesterday's ghost, her eyes intense, watery, and her lips barely parted. Her voice was deep and serious, touched here and there with a southern accent.

She looked at me again like she wanted to kill me, but more than before. She wanted to spit on me, and tar and feather me, and ride me out on a rail. "You talking about Chastity?"

"God, I hope not." My cigarette fell out of my fingers onto the bar. I felt very sorry. Sorry was writing itself all over me, but I don't think Donna saw it. She stepped back slowly. The glass made broken glass noises as she did so.

She leaned back on the counter and looked from me to Jessie. "I'm the one who found that girl's body. You think it's a joke, a funny story?"

My alien started screaming.

Jessica watched us, frozen. She eyed me eyeing Donna.

Donna walked over and picked up Chastity's funeral donation cup like it was a sick baby. She set it between us. "Why'd you move this? Didn't want to look at it?"

"I had no idea," came out of my mouth in a croaking whisper. "I didn't mean to . . ." How the hell was I supposed to know? I was twenty miles away from where it happened. There were only two other people in the bar. What were the fucking chances?

Donna tapped the cup. "I helped raise that girl. She my best friend's baby. Then she got in with that no-good low-life bum." She shoved the cup forward. "Feel like making a donation, New York?"

"Wait a minute," Jessica laid her hands flat on the table. "How do you know she's even talking about the same person? Let's calm down. She didn't know her. She just met this guy who told her—"

"Shhhh," I hissed at Jessica.

Donna did not like this. "Who told her what?" she demanded, stepping closer. "*Where'd* she meet this guy? You know where that bum is?"

Everything was like a bad train coming off a bad track right at my head. I started hacking up a storm. I couldn't breathe suddenly. It sounded like a herd of alien hell-puppies. Without moving from where she stood, Donna grabbed the cayenne pepper next to Jessica's drink and dumped some in my whiskey. Then she took my cigarette that was burning up her bar and dropped it in my water.

"Drink that," she told me, referring to the newly cayenned whiskey. "It'll loosen up your chest." Was she trying to kill me? "Go ahead. You're getting a little green around the edges," she pressed.

What the hell. I picked it up and gulped it down; whiskey and cayenne pepper. It burned everything. I gasped and sputtered. My chest rattled, then settled. My beast did feel freer, but I didn't know if that was a good thing. I smacked my lips and rubbed my eyes. "Damn!"

"You want some water?" Donna asked. I nodded yes. She nodded yes back. She didn't get me any water.

"I found her body and those texting messages. I showed them to the cops, 'cause I felt like they were like, her suicide note, you know?" Donna didn't look like she was going to cry. Her jaw was stiff and square. She was a toughie. My eyes were tearing up, though, bright red, I'm sure, and my throat and mouth burned like hell. I kept swallowing and sputtering. Donna tapped the funeral donation jar. I took out my wallet, produced a twenty and dropped it in. She nodded, turned around, and swiveled back with a glass of water for me. I drank the entire glass in five gulps. "What'd you say your name was, again?" I just shook my head no. She looked to Jessica. "You have *any idear* where he's hiding?"

Jessica picked up her purse and took me by the shoulder. Childhood friends can almost always be counted on in a pinch. "I'm sorry. I think we had better get going now." I felt half alive. Jessica helped me along my way. The old man at the bar was just staring at us trying to figure out what was going on. Donna's lips quivered, like Not-cousin's earlier that night. "It ain't right what happened. They're gonna find him with or without you," Donna kept on as we backed out the door. "We just want some answers!" she hollered. The door shut behind us.

I wheezed all the way to the car. "I see what you mean about having a weird night," Jessica said, propping me against the hood as she unlocked the passenger door. "I'm driving you to where you're staying. You're not in good shape."

My throat felt like an atomic bomb went off in a sandpaper factory. "What are the fucking chances?" I bellowed out. "That was weird. Don't you think that was *weird?*"

She nodded and half smiled at how horribly obvious the answer to my question was. I bent over and hacked. Something big moved inside of me. "Yes. That was one of the weirdest nights I've ever had. I just want us to get out of here," she told me, searching for her keys. "That was awful."

"It's too much of a coincidence," I kept on. "What the fuck is happening? It's like they planted her in there."

"They?"

I pounded on my chest, then balanced with my hands on my knees, groaning and beginning to convulse. "I don't know what I mean," I coughed out. "It just feels like someone is engineering everything."

"This is a small county, that's all."

"No. This is just too much. If I wrote this, no one would believe it." I let myself go into a coughing fit for a second and regained my breath. "*I* can't even believe it. Can you?"

The passenger side door was open. Jessica was standing next to it, staring at me with the most awful look on her face, her keys held tightly in her hands. "You look really bad. You look . . . green."

"What?" I hung my head over the black tar and coughed again. A little piece of mucus flew out of my mouth, landing on the ground in front of me. Jessica stepped back. Something rattled inside of me. I felt like I was going to explode. The mucus was green and slimy, reflecting the light from the bar sign. My chest heaved. I covered my mouth with my hand and took off running, doubled over, thinking I was going to vomit. That fucking cayenne whiskey bitch did me in.

I made it around to the back of the building. Holding onto the brick wall with one hand, the other on the dumpster, I let myself go with the reverent acquiescence of a drunken vomiter who has no choice but to let the void grab hold of her and show her how to make something out of nothing.

But what was coming out wasn't coming from my stomach. That thing in my chest, it was shaking itself free. It rumbled and screeched and pushed forward. My mouth wrenched itself open as wide as it could go. I felt a giant ball of slimy gum, slug-like, birthing itself through my facial orifice. It wiggled, elongated, and squeezed. It just kept coming out. I moaned loudly. I pounded the wall and heaved. It finally landed on the ground in front of me with a horrible plop.

I fell back on my ass and stared at it. It did not stare back. It didn't have eyes. It wiggled up against the wall and it squealed. The thing was green and slimy, like a green miniature version of the Blob. I moaned again. It started having some kind of seizure. Green slime and mucus and I guess my infected snot was flying off of it. As it shook itself free of my infected bronchitis placenta, it became visibly lighter and its glowing grew brighter. It began to become beautiful and it began to ascend.

It was a little wobbly at first, like a baby bird trying out its first feathers, but soon enough, it was going up, above the roof of the bar, my very own green glowing orb floating up there above the trees in that beautiful dark and twinkling country sky. I heard Jessica scream. A few counts later, I heard the sound of her engine revving and the screeching of tires against pavement.

I watched my orb for a good while. It was just hovering there, about forty feet directly above me. Then, over the trees lining the little houses, I saw another green form rising. It was faint at first, but it quickly grew clearer. The green light was a very familiar shape. I squinted. It kept approaching at about the same height as my glowing green orb. I cocked my head. It was that goddamned moldy couch. I heard muffled voices. That goddamned couch was glowing green and flying around above the town. On either side of the couch were two more green glowing orbs. That couch and its two green orbs flew up right next to my green orb and parked itself. The muffled voices revealed their faces, Little-little poked his head over the side of the glowing couch that was hovering above me, his feet dangling off the end. "Aw hell," he shouted. "Lookie there. It's my sister."

Not-cousin poked his head over the other side. "Hey there. You got one of those green balls, too!" he hollered, not as a question. "How do we lower this thing?" I heard him ask Little-little.

"Going down," I heard a voice say. This voice was deep and goofy like a children's cartoon character.

The couch and the orbs descended. I rose to my feet. Little-little sat on the glowing green couch hovering a few feet above the ground. The three glowing orbs bounced off each other sweetly, as a greeting. Little-little smiled his peachy keen smile at me. He still hadn't found a shirt he liked, I guess. "Hey, sis. We went into the woods and we found these fucking things. They're great. I think they were ours already."

I nodded, understanding.

"You coming?"

I looked around myself. "Where are you going?"

"We're heading to a non-extradition state," Not-cousin told me proudly.

"Nah, I'm voting for Mexico," Little-little came back.

The couch shivered. "All aboard that's coming aboard," the couch said.

The green orbs started circling. Not-cousin and Little-little held out their hands. I put my hands in theirs. They pulled me up, sitting me in between them. Little-little looked so happy. "I sure am stoked you're coming with us, sis. I miss ya, you know?" I put my arm around him. He laid his head on my shoulder, like he always used to do when he was really, really little. The green orbs spun faster around the couch, beginning the ascension once more.

We hit about seventy feet and started flying like condors, the towns streaking past, far below. The clouds were clearing. The stars were coming out, twinkling brighter. There's nothing like a country sky.

"To your left, notice Central Point, home of the Redhawks. In the nineteen thirties Central Point was a booming mecca for traveling businessmen and tradespeople, as the railroad provided the perfect midpoint for those traveling from Chicago to the southern states. The town to your right is Little Egypt and we will be coming upon Cairo soon, home of the Fighting Pharaohs, and known for being home to the largest manmade lake in the country," the couch told us in its goofy cartoon voice. That couch had turned out to be a world-class tour guide, after all.

Not-cousin watched the green orbs circling us, with amazement.

"East or west?" Little-little asked.

"I don't care."

"We can drop you off in New York first, if you want," Little-little told me. "Did you hear they got bin Laden? We heard it on the scanner."

I nodded. "Yep. I heard."

"Maybe we should go to Ground Zero," Not-cousin suggested. "There's a huge fucking party there."

"In this thing? They'd shoot us down." I patted Little-little's head. "Forget about New York. New York doesn't exist. It doesn't even have a sky."

Little-little took a pack of cigarettes out of his pocket. "I'm glad you said that. Still, I'd like to see it sometime. Big Apple." He offered me one if his cigarettes.

"Give me the pack," I said. He gave me the pack. I chucked it over the side and watched it spiral down to the cornfields of Central Point. "I think we've had enough." Little-little nodded and chucked his last smoke over the side, too.

"West it is," he said.

"West it is," the couch answered. The three spinning green orbs twisted around, circling west.

ZOMBIE

We always went down there where the dead left us alone. The cemetery was close to both of our houses. We could hop on our bikes and each make it there in ten minutes, tops, and there was no one there to keep us from doing whatever we wanted. Beth only had to travel down a quiet country road for about a mile. From my house, I had to get on the highway, make it past the truck stop and all the semis coming in to weigh or refill or sleep, then take a jog down a hill onto the unmarked back road, past some woods and cornfields, and then, there it was, the old cemetery, which sprawled out from the gated drive, expanding all the way back to the field.

A wooden fence divided the oldest section of the cemetery

from the newer burials, although the entire thing wasn't used much at all anymore. It looked like a puzzle, the way it was divided up. In the old section, tombstones were dated all the way back to the early 1700s, with worn-out granite that looked exhausted from keeping up the memory. Most of the tombstones looked like they wanted to let everyone finally forget and move on. Rain-worn, it was difficult to make out the names and the exact dates. You could intuit the information from what was left of the letters: an *M*, an *R*, maybe the hint of a *Y* was obviously Mary, and she died either in 1762 or 1785, or something close to that.

We preferred the cemetery to the park or the school sports grounds. There were no other kids at the cemetery to bug us. At the park, kids were always poking at me, trying to pick a fight with me, saying I was ugly and saying I looked like a dude, or chasing Beth around; the girls calling her a slut and boys trying to get her to kiss them, and we could never get anything fun done at the park. That's why we ended up playing in the cemetery after school, which didn't really help either of us where popularity was concerned. On top of everything else, we soon became known as the weird girls who hung out in the cemetery all the time.

Because of our weirdnesses compounded on top of weirdnesses, all we really had was each other, until she came into our lives. Then we had each other and we had *her*, but it felt like we had so much more than that.

I never knew a person could live like that; well, not really live, but *survive* like that. It made me feel like anything was possible. There's something very particular about having a secret that big when you're twelve years old. You get to live in two different worlds, and whatever is happening in the normal world can't really touch you, because you have this other world you can go into, where everything is so much more amazing and unbelievable. It's easy to keep worlds separate at that age, because you're straddling childhood and adulthood. You're already living on the edge of reality and fantasy, and just barely growing out of pretending all the time.

But this secret world wasn't pretend; it was something else that, like a pretend world, would shatter as soon as it was integrated into normal life. At first, like a fantasy, it supplemented, but soon, because it was real, it supplanted our boring reality. The secret world became the most real, and the world we lived in every day with everyone else became something we had to get through to get back to *her*.

It was nearing the end of September. We'd been back in school long enough to have almost forgotten the freedom of summer. It must have been a weekend, because I was spending the night at Beth's house, which meant we got to stay out till after dusk.

We went to the cemetery right after school. I put some music on my boom box. I liked to be retro, and listened to actual CDs of Godsmack, and Siouxsie and the Banshees, and Nine Inch Nails, and other good music that only happened in generations before me, and we played catch, and knocked a softball around with our bats, and had a picnic. We messed around all day. Then night fell, and we decided to play flashlight tag. This might not sound that entertaining with only two people, but in a cemetery at night, it was a lot of fun. Whoever was "it" would close her eyes for a count of twenty, and the other person would run and hide behind one of the many tombstones or trees in the sprawling graveyard. The one hiding would shriek ghostly noises, which, if done right, would echo and throw the seeker onto the wrong track. When Beth was tagged, she would jump out squealing, and hold her hands up like claws and rush at me. We liked to scare ourselves silly.

It was the second round of flashlight tag. We'd been screeching up a storm of fake horror since the sun set. Beth was "it." I ran far away from her and crouched behind a headstone at the edge of the cemetery grounds near the field. It was very dark, save for the light of the moon, and a streetlamp a nearby farmer had mounted in his yard. The light shone through the wooded area that lined the south side of the cemetery, the blue light splitting through the leaves like spectral stars. Beth called out, "I'm coming for you," her flashlight beam bouncing in the distance, pointing nowhere near where I was hiding. I kept silent, peeking over the top of a tombstone. Beth called out again, "I'm coming for you, creep!" I screeched. It echoed. She stopped and circled her light around the graveyard, and then, for some inexplicable reason, she started running in the opposite direction of where I was hiding. She ran away from me, shouting, "I see you! I see you!" I stood to get a better look, wondering how she could be so mistaken. She pointed her light in the very wrong direction in which she was also running, and, to my astonishment, it caught a figure of what seemed to be a person. This person halted momentarily, then quickly dashed through an open area, and hid behind a tree near the Thompson Mausoleum. "Hey, I got you. I tagged you. Come out! You're *it* now," Beth demanded. A chill shot through me. We weren't alone.

I stood up, waving my arms frantically, "Beth! Beth, I'm over here," I shouted from far behind her. Beth stopped, frozen in place, turned and shined her light on me, then she shined it back to where the figure she'd tagged was crouching behind a tree. Beth screamed, then took off in a dead run back to where I was standing.

"There's someone else here! There's someone else here, Gillian," she panted when she got to me. I threw my arm around her shoulder, and pulled my flashlight out of my back pocket. We both pointed our lights toward where Beth had been standing. "Who's there? We've got a gun," I shouted, deepening my voice, trying to sound tough, and older. Beth raised her eyebrows at me.

"Why'd you say that?" she asked.

"I don't want them to think they can fuck with us," I told her.

"Maybe it was an animal," she said, continuing to scan the cemetery with her flashlight. Right then, something moved near her beam. She caught it with her light and followed it. It was definitely a person, dashing toward the mausoleum, and then, miraculously, the person opened the mausoleum door and disappeared inside. We both turned our flashlights off and crouched down. "What do we do?" Beth whispered.

"I don't know. Maybe we should just leave." I felt totally terrified.

"Do you think it's alive?" she asked.

I turned to get a look at her. "What are you talking about? Of course they're alive. They were running, weren't they?"

"No." She looked at me like I was stupid. "I mean, what if it's, like, a ghost?"

"A ghost wouldn't show up in the light, would it? I mean, wouldn't a ghost, like, be transparent?" Sometimes Beth didn't think things through.

She shook her head, pondering. "What if it's a zombie?"

I looked around the cemetery for any signs of the dead beginning to dig their way up through the dirt to herald what I suddenly believed to be the inevitable zombie apocalypse that, somewhere deep inside, I always knew was coming. "If it *is* a zombie," I said, "we have to stop it. It just takes one, and then they bite someone, then they bite someone else, and then it's all over."

"Right," Beth nodded solemnly.

"We've got to kill it," I said, feeling a childish bravery take over.

"How are we going to kill it? What are you talking about?" Beth balked. "We're not big enough to kill anyone."

"Sure we are. There are two of us, and we have bats."

"But they're all the way over there." She pointed to where we'd left the bats, next to the boom box, just a few yards away from the mausoleum.

"Let's go get them. Just stay close to me," I instructed. "And remember, you have to hit zombies in the head. The only way to kill a zombie is to destroy its head, because the infection is in the brain."

"How do you know that?" Beth asked.

"I read a lot," I told her, and tugged at her sleeve to move. We made our way stealthily through the cemetery, crouching and scurrying, then stopping to hide behind a tombstone every few feet and peeking around to make sure that who or whatever it was who went in hadn't come back out of the mausoleum, though it was hard to tell for sure in the dark. We finally made it to our bats. Beth told me to take the aluminum bat and that she would take the wooden one since I was stronger and it would do more damage. We argued over whether that was logical. Since she was weaker, I thought she should have the more durable bat, for added protection. But finally, she had it her way, like she always did when we argued.

I gripped my bat with two hands, and told her to keep her flashlight off and only to turn it on when I gave the word. I crept up to the mausoleum, taking one careful step after another, Beth right behind me. There were only three mausoleums in the whole cemetery. There weren't many wealthy families in the town. It was a lot for most people just to afford a headstone. This one was the nicest and the largest mausoleum of the few of them. It was about the size of a small storage shed, made of gray stone, and adorned with two lion's heads flanking the top of the doorway, ringed by chiseled flora.

When we got to the door, we could see very clearly that the lock had been broken. The chain hung loose off the metal handle, which I took hold of and, after taking a deep breath, pulled open. I jumped into the doorway, like I was in an action movie, my bat raised over my head, and shouted, "Now!" Beth turned on her flashlight and shined it past me into the small stone room.

"Ahhhhh!" I heard someone shriek. The light illuminated the inside of the mausoleum, and I saw her. She held her hands over her head and cowered down on the far wall. I swung my bat in front of myself twice, hollering, "Get back! Get back!" But she wasn't moving, except to cover her head with her hands. "Get up! Get up and put your hands up!" I demanded. But she just continued to cover her head and assumed a fetal position on the floor against the wall.

"Who are you?" Beth shouted at her, her voice trembling with fear. I was shaking too, and didn't know what to do. She seemed to be a skinny, very human woman. She was wearing hot pink cutoff shorts, and had dirty, stringy blond hair. That was all I could really tell, because of the way she was curled up. There were a couple of open scratches and some small sores on her legs and arms, and because of that, she did look like she *might* be a zombie, but the way she was cowering had me seriously questioning that possibility.

"Don't hurt me. Please. I'm sorry. I'm sorry," she moaned. "I didn't do *anything*!"

"Get up!" I told her again. "Stand up so I can see you, and put your hands up, too." I was proud of how authoritative I sounded.

"Okay, okay. Just don't hurt me." She uncurled herself and put her hands up, then clumsily came to a standing position. She didn't look like the undead necessarily, but then, it wasn't completely a sure thing, because she looked closer to dead than any living person I'd ever seen.

She was very thin, and her skin had a pale, grayish hue to it that did not allay my morbid fears. Her makeup was all smeared and fucked up. Her blue eyeshadow was smudged weirdly, and her bright red lipstick was smeared along her lips so that it jutted off to the side of her face. I couldn't tell her age. She could have been thirty, forty, or fifty. I had no idea. She wore an old T-shirt with a silhouette of a bird on it that said "Birdie's Gonna Fly," and, like I said before, cutoff hot pink shorts and white sneakers. She squinted in the glare of Beth's light, which was aimed directly at her face. "What do you want from me? Just take it. Take whatever you want," she pleaded.

Beth and I looked to each other for an answer. We didn't have any answer. Beth pointed her flashlight around the cold cement room. There was a stone bench attached to the wall that was covered in a collection of stained blankets and pillows. A large box sat across from the makeshift bed, obviously being used as a table. On top of it was a half-eaten Snickers bar, several candles, a mirror and razor, a glass pipe, a lighter, a pack of cigarettes, an open can of Mountain Dew, and some potato chips. On the floor was a tattered backpack, a pile of clothes, a box of incense, and a half-full bottle of vodka. The place looked like a weird nest.

From above us, embedded in the wall, a stained-glass Virgin Mary looked down on us, and lining the wall were plaques with the names of the people whose bodies rested, I supposed, inside the walls of the mausoleum.

She bent forward, as the light was no longer in her eyes, and got a better look at us. "Hey, wait a minute. You're just some kids." She started to put her hands down.

"Watch it!" I shouted, raising my bat higher, trying to seem menacing. "Keep them up!" She put them back up, but seemed less intimidated.

"You little girls?" she asked. "Two little girlies?"

"Are you alive?" Beth asked, shining her flashlight back in the woman's face.

"Am I alive? What the hell kinda question is that? Course I'm alive. Aw, did I scare y'all?"

"We ain't scared," I told her. "You're the one that oughta be scared."

"Okay, okay. Don't whack me, honey. I ain't done nothing to you. Here. I got something for you." She slowly crouched down and reached toward her bag with one of her shaking, skinny hands. "Here, let's be friends." She squatted lower and fished around her backpack. "Here, I got a peace offering." She reached into a pocket of the bag with one hand, keeping the other one in the air, and pulled out a Hershey's bar. She held it up to us. "Here you go. You girlies want a candy bar?"

"No thank you," Beth responded instinctually.

"Shh!" I snapped at her, giving her an exasperated look. That was no way to talk to a hostage.

"Sorry, gosh," Beth muttered.

"Maybe I got something else you'd like." Now both of her hands were down and she was just rummaging around her backpack.

"Hey now. You'll let a poor little lady have a cigarette, won't you?" she asked, feigning being very pitiful, tilting her head up at me.

"I guess," I said, feeling I was losing my grip on the situation.

She produced a lighter from the bag and stood, then slowly reached for the pack of cigarettes on the makeshift table. "Thanks, honey. That's mighty kind of you." She took out a cigarette and lit it. "Let's get a little light on this subject. Whatdya say?" She proceeded to light the many candles on the "table," then she sat on her "bed" and puffed her cigarette, regarding us with curiosity. Beth and I looked to each other in confusion. I slowly let the bat down, but kept it in my grip, resting it on my shoulder, just in case. Beth turned off her flashlight and rested her bat with its tip on the ground.

"Who are you?" I asked. "Are you *living* in here?"

"Who are *you*?" she retorted.

"I'm Beth. This is Gillian," Beth told her politely. I rolled my eyes. What had gotten into her?

"I'm Tanya. Nice to meet you." She held out her hand to shake and, to my horror, Beth shook it. Beth had the weirdest look on her face. She had kept letting a smile bloom, then trying to fix it back to a poker face, but it was obvious she was bursting with giddy excitement. "What are you two doing out here so late?" Tanya asked.

"This is where we hang out," Beth said.

"What are you doing here, inside this . . . place?" I asked, my tone not at all friendly. It bothered me that Beth was acting so immediately taken by this strange woman.

She shrugged, took another drag of her cigarette, and ashed it on the floor. "Seems like as good a place as any," she said. "Oh, I'm sorry. I'm being rude. You want one?" She held the pack of cigarettes out to us.

"We are *not* old enough," I told her insistently.

"Well, I'm not calling the police. Are you?" Tanya smiled up at Beth and winked. To my dismay, Beth giggled.

"Go ahead," Tanya pressed. Beth laid her bat down, walked over to her and took a cigarette out of the pack.

"*I'll* try it, Gillian. I always wanted to." Beth was acting like this was some cool high school party we'd been privileged enough to gain access to. She sat down next to Tanya and put the cigarette in her mouth. Tanya lit it for her. She inhaled, suppressed a cough, and let it out as coolly as possible. "Mmm," she said, holding herself like she was much older, her shoulders back, her legs crossed. "It tastes like peppermints." She let the cigarette dangle from her fingers and looked around the tomb. "Cool setup you have here," she told Tanya.

"Thanks." Tanya looked me up and down. "Now, I woulda guessed that *she* was the do-goody," she motioned to Beth, "and *you* was the bad influence. But I guess looks can be deceiving." Beth laughed at that, too.

"She's brave," she told Tanya, "but she don't like to get in trouble."

"That right?" Tanya asked. "You sure do look like you'd be the one to instigate."

I knew what she meant. I looked like a tomboy, and I dressed weird. I wore almost all black. I dressed like a cartoon character back then; basically the same outfit every day. I always wore a black baseball cap over my short black hair. Dad wouldn't let me cut it as short as I wanted, so I had it cut in a bob, just above my chin. He let me dye it, though, and it was jet black, and so was my T-shirt, and so were my high-top sneakers, but my shorts were almost always blue jeans, and went no shorter than just above my knee. Beth, on the other hand, looked like a regular girl. She was blond and pretty, and wore whatever: jeans and cute shorts and blouses and girl's T-shirts, and even dresses. She wore makeup when she could get away with it, and kept her hair neatly combed or in a cute little ponytail on top of her head. Of the two of us, she definitely looked like she would be the one less likely to get into trouble.

"Do *you* want to try it? It's nice." Beth held the cigarette up to me, a weirdly excited look in her eyes.

"Whatever," I said, and took the cigarette nonchalantly. I sucked on it. It stung like hell. I sputtered and those two giggled at me. I handed it back to Beth, patting at my chest. "That's horrible," I coughed out. It made me immediately dizzy and nauseated. To this day I cannot stand the taste of menthols. I paced around the small cement enclosure. "Do you . . . *live* here?" I asked again.

Tanya sniffed hard and wiped her nose with her arm. "For now." She looked up at me, and pinched up her face. "I'm not gonna lie. I'm in hiding. My husband," she said, flicking her cigarette again, "he's been beating me bad, and I gotta hide out from him right now. You understand?"

"Oh gosh," Beth looked very sad and worried for her. "*Beating* you?"

"Yeah, he's a jealous motherfucker." She talked loud and fast when she talked about this. "He says, 'Tanya, what you doin' with those guys down at the bar?' And I ain't doin' nothin' with no one. Just go have a drink with my girlfriends. What can I do if other men talk to us? But he thinks I'm always getting with every guy in town. And when I come home, he knocks me around. I couldn't take it no more. I took off. That'll show him. I decided to hole up here for a while, till I can work out a plan."

"Oh god. I'm so sorry." Beth shook her head and took another drag of her own cigarette, but I think it was a fake drag. I don't think she was inhaling anymore, because she wasn't even coughing.

"Oh honey, it's awful," Tanya went on. "Last month, I told him I was pregnant with his baby. And the old fool didn't believe it was his, so he . . ." She paused and looked at Beth for signs of emotion. Beth was listening, entranced, and apparently growing very concerned. "He done beat it outa me. Beat that unborn baby, dead, he sure did." She was talking a mile a minute. "Beat the damned thing right outa me." She made a punching motion toward her stomach and doubled over. "I lost that baby, and that's when I took off. I need . . . I need help, girls."

I stood over them, also stunned from her story, my mouth actually hanging open. "He killed your baby?" I whispered in astonishment.

"Jesus!" Beth let out. "Do you want us to call the police? Gillian!" Beth tugged on my shirt. "We can call the police for her."

"No police!" Tanya hollered, loudly. We stared at her silently, startled by her response. She placed her hand on Beth's shoulder. "You just can't. Okay?"

"Why not?" Beth asked shyly. "Isn't that what you're supposed to do?"

"No. No. See . . ." She seemed to be searching for words. "The truth is, all the police, well . . . they're his buddies. They'll just believe his side, and they'll tell him where I am. You can't call the police. That ain't what I need. I need to keep hiding. No one can know I'm here, you understand?" She was very intense about this point. We both nodded in agreement.

"Okay," I agreed.

"It's gotta be a secret. A lot of people know my boyfriend, and if anyone finds out—"

"I thought you said it was your husband," I interrupted.

"What?" She shook her head. "Same difference. Oh god. This all gets me so upset and confused, talkin' about this." Beth patted Tanya on the back. Her cigarette was burned down. She followed Tanya's lead and dropped it on the floor and stepped on it. "I need a drink." Tanya said. She stood and picked up the vodka bottle, poured a bunch of it into the open can of Mountain Dew, then took a big swig. "Ahhh." She smacked her lips, happily. "That's better." She held out the can of vodka Mountain Dew. "You want some?"

Beth and I looked at each other in shock. I felt terrified the way children do when they don't know they're terrified. Beth's expression was stunned too, but excitement quickly began dancing in her eyes, and I could almost hear her thinking, *Come on, Gillian. Do you want to do it? Let's do it. Let's drink that vodka Mountain Dew.* Our parents had always told us never to take candy from strangers. They obviously had not thought about how much more enticing the offer of our first taste of cigarettes and liquor might be.

I shook my head. "I'm not old enough," I told Tanya.

"Is that right?" Tanya said, taking another swig of her "cocktail."

"It's late," I told Beth. "Your mom's going to come looking for us if we don't go back soon."

"You two live nearby?" Tanya asked.

"Just down the road," Beth told her. I elbowed her. I began to think maybe Beth's parents had never told her *anything* about talking to strangers.

Tanya raised an eyebrow at that. "Oh yeah? Down *this* road?"

"Mmmm-hmmm," Beth nodded.

"How'd you two like to make five dollars?"

"For what?" I asked.

Tanya came and sat down next to Beth. "I ain't had hot food in days. I'm so hungry, girls. If you could find any way to bring me any kind of hot food later tonight, or even tomorrow, I'd pay you for it. Five dollars. Easy as pie." She took out another cigarette and lit it. "If you come back later tonight, we could have ourselves a little party. Whatdya say? A secret slumber party, just us girls?"

I shook my head again. "I don't know if we can do that."

"But . . . *maybe*," Beth said eagerly. "We could try, maybe, couldn't we, Gillian?"

"It sure would mean the world to me. I've been out here all alone with no company, and all."

I picked up Beth's bat and grabbed her by the elbow. "Let's go, before we get in trouble."

"She's right," Tanya said. "Don't want your parents coming out here looking for y'all."

Beth stood and looked at Tanya intently. "We'll help you," she said. "I promise." A sort of chill gripped me when she said that.

"You're a real sweetheart," Tanya told her.

I waved goodbye to Tanya. She waved back. We pushed open the mausoleum door and stepped out into the dark country night.

We packed our things into the basket on my bike and rode back to Beth's house. She was so excited about our weird discovery, she was all hopped up on adrenaline and going a mile a minute. The whole way biking home, she kept hollering at me how amazing it all was. "Can you believe it?" She went on and on. "She *lives* in there. In the cemetery! She is so cool. This is so awesome. I mean, it's awful what happened to her, but it's kind of cool, right?"

I didn't say much. I wasn't sure whether it was very cool. I felt slightly scared of, and overwhelmingly sorry for, the woman. Beth asked me if we were going to sneak out and go back, but in a way that made it clear that she would be very disappointed if we didn't. She'd also become fixated on the idea of trying liquor for the first time. Drinking liquor had never been suggested to us before. But now that it was a clear possibility, it seemed like it was all she'd ever really wanted to do. Through the entirety of our thus-far lifelong friendship, I somehow had no idea that Beth's greatest ambition in life was simply to one day get drunk. Apparently the company and context mattered not. I didn't dare stand in the way of this tween rite of passage.

It was horribly easy to sneak out of her parents' house. They both worked six days a week in the car parts factory, and woke at five in the morning, even on Saturdays, which meant they went to bed at around ten. When we got back to Beth's house, we put a frozen pizza in the oven and turned on the TV. An hour later, her parents told us good night and not to stay up too late. Beth packed up the food with all the care of a mother packing her child's lunch for their first day of school. We took the pizza out of the oven and sliced it up. She wrapped it in tinfoil so that the slices would stay warm, reminding me that Tanya had specifically requested *hot* food. Then she heated a can of chicken noodle soup in the microwave and poured it into her mother's thermos. I grabbed some chips and a couple of sodas. We didn't even have to sneak out the window or anything. We went through the front door, and made it back to the cemetery just before eleven.

It was a strange thing to knock on a mausoleum door, and even more so to do it expecting an answer. Tanya opened the door and let us in. "I didn't think you'uns would really come back," she said excitedly.

"We brought you food, *hot* food, like you asked for," Beth told her, proudly holding out the thermos. "We brought hot soup and pizza."

"Oh my gosh, golly. Thank you so much," Tanya said, waving her hand in the air. She was smoking a cigarette, again. She seemed to be a chain smoker, and the small room was thick with it. She propped the door open to let it air out, then went to her bag and got out five singles. "Here you go, girlies, just like I promised." Beth started to decline the money, but I took the five dollars, telling her it was no problem. Tanya took the thermos, unscrewed the lid, and started drinking the soup, *mmm'ing* and *aaahhh'ing*, and she gulped half of it down. "Damn, that's good!" she exclaimed, wiping her lips.

There's something very satisfying about feeding a hungry person. After she had enough soup, she made a spot for us on her makeshift bed and piled some pillows on the floor where she sat at our feet. She asked if we wanted to listen to music, and turned on a small battery-powered radio. It just played the local country station, but it was fine. She asked for the pizza. Beth got out the aluminum-wrapped slices. We each took one. I opened two sodas for us. It was just like any other slumber party I'd ever been to, except it was being hosted by a homeless adult, and we were in a cemetery hiding in a candlelit one-room mausoleum. And also, the menthol smoke that hung in the air.

After Tanya took her third bite of pizza and thanked us for the tenth time, Beth began to get fidgety. I could tell she had her mind on one thing, and one thing only, but was too mannered to ask for it. Tanya, while eating the pizza, kept taking big gulps of what appeared to be a fresh Mountain Dew, which, I guessed from her demeanor, also contained a fair amount of vodka. Beth eyed it longingly. I took notice of the previously half-full bottle of vodka that sat by the box/table. It was now nearly empty. I felt both disappointment and relief at the thought that we were probably not going to be getting drunk for the first time that night. "Damn this pizza is good," she went on, before taking another bite. "Dang. Pepperoni?"

"Yes. Pepperoni."

"Dang."

She finished her slice and asked for another. Beth gave her another. "I don't usually eat," she said, "but hot pizza sure is yummy. You start to miss hot food after a few days. That bastard got me out here with nothing real to eat, and all."

I thought the statement "I don't usually eat" was odd. Beth finally noticed the mostly empty bottle of vodka and I could see by the look on her face that her heart was completely sunk when she saw it. Without the vodka, I supposed, it wasn't much of a party for her. We were just sitting in a mausoleum with a homeless woman, feeding her hot food, listening to her talk about her abusive husband, or boyfriend or whatever. Without the vodka, it was more like social work than a secret slumber party, really.

But then Tanya asked, "Hey, girlies, you want a little something extra in your sodas?"

Beth shrugged like she hadn't thought of it. "Well, you don't really have much left, do you?"

"What? Sure I do. Just get under the bed there you're sitting on." Beth's eyes lit up. We both leaned over, looking under the stone bench she'd covered in blankets and called a bed, where she'd stashed another full bottle of vodka, as well as a nearly full bottle of whiskey. They were shiny and commanding.

We drank the vodka. It was clear and nearly tasteless, except for the burn that bad vodka has. It made the Mountain Dew sizzle like an electric jolt.

Thirty minutes later, Tanya was dancing. She was shimmying and twirling, and once, she leapt, like a strange, scrawny, drunk ballerina. Beth was laughing at her, and I felt brave and excited and confused. We were loud. We were screaming and howling. The walls were full of the dead and we were drunk children shrieking at them.

Tanya clapped her hands and tried to sing along with the music on the radio, "His shitty little soaped-up four-wheel drive . . . yow!" This suddenly caused her to lose her breath and begin a very serious coughing fit. When it was over, she sat down and gave us a cheers with her soda can. She told us she liked us. Beth said she felt dizzy and lay down, resting her head on my lap. I felt a little dizzy as well, and the vodka burned my throat and stomach every time I took a drink, but I liked that feeling.

Tanya said it was time to take her medicine. She picked something up off the table, then dug around in her bag and walked over to the window ledge. I wasn't paying her much attention. I was twirling Beth's hair and she was humming along to the song on the radio, holding her soda-can cocktail so it rested on her chest and she could lift her head and take a swig whenever she got the urge. I heard Tanya snorting loudly. Her back was turned to us. She was sniffing something and wiping her nose.

"What's that?" Beth asked her.

"It's my sinus medicine," Tanya told her. She walked away from the window and sat back down near us. "What do you want to do now?" she asked excitedly.

"What else *is* there to do?" Beth asked, looking around the tiny room with its close, cold stone walls, the names of the dead etched into its smooth bricks.

"We could play games," Tanya chirped.

"Like board games?" Beth asked, unimpressed.

"No, like drinking games," Tanya came back.

"I don't know what that means." I shook my head. I was feeling a bit hazy. "Drinking games?"

"Yeah," Tanya explained. "There's one where you say something you've never done, and whoever has done it, they gotta take a drink. Then you know what they did, and you also get more drunk."

"Oh, it sounds kinda like skeletons in the closet," Beth said. "I love that game."

"You have booze left?" Tanya asked.

Beth held up her can. "It's half full."

"That's mostly soda, though. Here, I'll give you some more." Tanya leaned forward and poured a bunch of vodka in Beth's can, then in mine. "Okay, now we can play. You start," she pointed to me. "Just say something you've never done."

"Ummm, okay." I shrugged. "I've never cut class." Beth and Tanya both took a drink.

Bore-ring! Beth sang, sitting up and adjusting herself on the "bed." "I've got a good one." She wiggled her eyebrows, and smirked evilly, but it was a strange, drunken smirk that seemed to be manifesting through a thick fog. "I've never . . ." she looked at both of us, drawing this statement out for dramatic effect, "had *sex*!?" she squealed, and covered her hand with her mouth, giggling.

Tanya took a big swig of her drink, meaning she'd had sex. Beth giggled harder. It was amazing. We'd never met an adult who didn't treat us like little kids. They treated us that way, of course, because we *were* little kids. But with her, we'd found an alternate dimension where being an adult and being a kid didn't mean what they were supposed to. She would tell us the truth. She was an adult and would tell us the truth about it, and we didn't have to act a certain way or watch what we said around her, or pretend not to know things we already knew, or pretend not to be curious about things we were curious about. "Did it hurt the first time? How old were you?" Beth was obviously very curious. She looked at me and hiccuped. "Oh my god, did you ever poot it in yer mouth?" She was wavering where she sat and had drunk enough that she was beginning to slur her words. My head felt very heavy, but also, somehow, like it was floating.

"NO! NO! NO!" Tanya screamed, clapping her hands in the air. "That ain't how you play. You get *one* turn! *One* turn."

"I'm sorry," Beth said, laying her head back against the wall and taking a deep breath.

"I'll tell you, though. But don't go outa turn again, okay?" Tanya was talking very fast and loud. "It hurts like hell. Yeah, girl! But it hurts even worse if it's your first time and you're not willing, so if that happens, just try and like it." Beth scrunched up her forehead and blinked, looking confused. My mouth, once again, fell open as Tanya went on. "And they *always, alllll waaays* want you to put it in your mouth. Hell, sometimes you can make 'em pay to do that or in your butt, even. They're crazy about it. Especially the truckers down there." She motioned in a direction that I understood to mean the truck stop down the road, between the cemetery and my house. "I don't know why they like it so much, but they do. Ha!" She let out a loud laugh and took a sip of her drink. "I worsh with Listerine after if I can, and," she pointed at Beth, "don't ever swallow that shit, no matter what they say." We stared at her blankly in stunned silence. Beth blinked a few times, trying to take in all the new information she'd just received. "Hey, how old are you, anyway?" Tanya asked Beth.

"I'm . . . eleven," Beth said meekly.

"I'm twelve," I said, taking a very small sip of my drink. "She'll be twelve too, next month. But I'll be thirteen in four months. We're in middle school. Sixth grade." I didn't know if this was important, but I worried that when Beth said "eleven" it had sounded too young, and we would get in trouble, somehow. Tanya, though, was unfazed.

"You look older than your age," she told Beth. "You're a pretty girl, so I'll tell you something." She paused to scratch a spot on her arm that looked as if it had been scratched many times before. "If a boy tells you size don't matter, it means he's got a little dinker. And it *does* matter."

"What?!" Beth let out, spitting her drink out of her mouth and across the floor. She covered her mouth with her hands and snorted, then buried her head in my shoulder, having a laughing fit. Tanya started laughing too, in a loud, booming "Ha, ha, ha!" and slapped her thigh. I patted Beth's head. Tears were running down her eyes from her laughter. It was a drunk, hysterical laughter that almost wouldn't stop. Tanya got up and went to the window and took more of her sinus medicine. Beth finally sat upright, took some deep breaths, and calmed herself down. "My stomach hurts from laughing," she told me, sighing exhaustedly. "Ohhhh wow."

Tanya sat back down on the floor. "It's my turn," she hollered, then sniffed loudly and tilted her head back and sniffed again. "Hey," she looked around, "where's my drink?" She looked at Beth. "Did you take my drink?" she shouted in a sudden outburst. "You don't gotta do that. I done give you your own. What the hell?" Beth meekly pointed to the small cement ledge below the stained-glass window where Tanya's Mountain Dew can sat. "Awww, damn." She stood and went back to the ledge to get her drink and immediately took a big gulp of it. "Oookay," she said, calming down. "My turn. Hmmm." She sucked on her bottom lip and looked from me to Beth, and back again. "I've never . . ." she eyed me weirdly and took a few steps toward us, "I've never . . . kissed a girl," she leaned down for effect, "with *tongue!*" She shouted, and stared at me pointedly. I shrugged and shook my head, narrowing my eyes. I didn't take a drink. Neither did Beth. But Tanya took a big drink of her "cocktail."

"Wait," I asked, "does that mean you *have* done it?"

"Hell yeah, honey," she said, wiping her mouth with her arm.

"But aren't you supposed to say things you *haven't* done?" Beth asked.

"It don't matter. You say whatever, and if you're lying, you have to drink. That way you can drink even when it's your turn," Tanya explained.

"But we've all been drinking anyway. It's just, when someone says something you've done, you also have to drink then, right?" I asked, incredulously.

"Who cares!" Tanya shouted and started laughing at me. "You are so uptight."

"Yeah, Gillian, don't be so uptight," Beth said, shoving me, playfully. She took a swig of her drink. I was feeling very drunk already, and Beth was drinking even more than me.

"I'm not uptight," I said, my expression sour. "I just want to know what the rules are." I let out a frustrated sigh and took a big drink of my cocktail. They were getting on my nerves. I felt a strange, burning anger rise suddenly from my burning stomach.

Beth rested her head in her hands and mumbled, "Is the room spinning?" Then she did her best to sit upright and giggled at nothing.

"I thought for sure you'd take a drink on that one," Tanya told me.

I didn't like this statement. I furrowed my eyebrows in her direction. "What the hell is that supposed to mean?"

"Oh, you know," Tanya said. "You just look like you would've, that's all."

Beth laughed at that.

I shoved her lightly with my hand. "Shut up," I told her.

"I'm sorry, Gillian," Beth said, snorting and trying not to laugh. "I'm sorry."

"You never even done it for practice?" Tanya asked, her eyes wide with excitement. She crossed over to us and sat back down. "I dare you'uns to."

"Dare us to what?" I asked.

"*Kiss!*" Tanya shouted. "Kiss! Kiss! Kiss!" She clapped her hands in rhythm to the words.

"Kiss *who*?" I squealed.

"Each other."

Beth looked at me, and laughed harder. She'd been on a drunk, long roller coaster of laughter for five straight minutes now. Sometimes it subsided, but was never fully gone, it was just a dip, where her laughter came to a brief rest, only to prepare for the next mounting crescendo of something that would push her over the edge, and she'd be sent rolling along the track of another outburst. She laughed and laughed and squealed, "Kiss me, Gillian!" and fell over.

"We're not *playing* truth or dare," I snapped at Tanya. "What the hell is wrong with you two?" This night foretold our drinking to come in years ahead. I was obviously an irritable, easily angered drunk, and Beth was the kind of drunk who might end up on a *Girls Gone Wild* video, constantly squealing and laughing at the absurd hilarity of, and game for, everything.

"Why not? Let's play truth or dare!" Tanya boomed excitedly. She smacked her thigh. "Come on. I dare you to kiss her. *With tongue.*"

Beth lay on her side, giggling, "Kiss me, Gillian. Pucker up!" she said, pawing at the air. "Kissy kissy. Hahaha." She was drunker than I was.

"Why do you get to go first?" I said to Tanya. "It would be our turn to say I never, so we should get the first dare." I let out a long, annoyed, hissing sigh.

"Fine," Tanya said. "Dare me. But if I do your dare, you got to do mine."

Beth sat back up, unsteadily. "You'll do a dare?" she asked, happily. She looked up at the ceiling. "Oh, oh I got one." She held her finger in the air like a cartoon scholar who just had a bright idea, then brought the finger down and pointed it at Tanya. Her words came out in one childishly eager, drunken stream. "I dare you to take off your clothes, down to your underwear, and run all out to the road and . . ." she thought too hard, "spin around, and dance, *naked*, and then run back."

"Can I keep my shoes on?" Tanya asked. Beth nodded yes, rubberly, and took another drink.

"You're not going to do that," I said.

"Hell yeah I am. We're having a party," Tanya retorted, standing and immediately removing her shirt. "But then, you gotta kiss her." Beth nodded in agreement again, her head falling down slowly, then quickly snapping up, her eyelids heavy and lips pursed in what I think she thought was a smile, but what was beginning to look more like an imitation of a duck gone wrong.

Tanya wasn't wearing a bra. Her breasts were small and her dark nipples were hard against the chill of early autumn. She struggled to get her tight shorts off over her tennis shoes, but soon enough she was standing before us in her baby blue cotton panties, waving her arms over her head, and enthusiastically hopping in place. "Let's do it!" she shouted. Beth and I followed her out of the mausoleum. As soon as she'd made it outside, she took off in a strange, wobbling, yet vigorous run down the dark gravel drive, screaming "Yeeehaaaaw!" and "Yow!" as she went. When she hit the road, she ran out to the middle and, topless, in her underwear and tennis shoes, began doing an erratic Twist and Mashed Potato, shining, pale and white, visible by the light of the nearly full moon.

The dancing in the road took longer than I believe Beth had intended, and I very much hoped a car wouldn't happen to pass as she was dancing her weird jig in the night, but finally, she deemed the deed done, and she ran back to us, stopping before us and panting, bent over with her hands on her knees like a woman who'd just finished a triathlon. "I did it," she panted, and held her hand up for a high five. I high-fived her.

"You did it," Beth squeaked happily, "you dud it." She was holding onto my arm with her extremely inebriated head resting against my shoulder. "Dud it," she squeaked again, leaning against me. "Dud ut, dud unt, dud dunt, did it, dunt dunt, dun dun." It was the Pink Panther theme song she was singing. When she was done, she giggled meekly and rubbed her head against the arm of my jacket.

"Okay." Tanya stood erect, amazingly unencumbered by being nearly naked in fifty degree weather. "You two's turn. You gotta do your dare now."

"We gotta do ur dare," Beth slurred, smiling up at me from my side.

"Fine," I said. I took her by the shoulders and turned her to face me.

"With tongue!" Tanya hollered.

She was watching us like we were the most intriguing film. Beth was having trouble standing on her own, still she persisted, smiling up at me with her heavy eyes and wobbling in place. "Kiss me, Gillian," she said like it was a joke, and puckered her lips. I sighed heavily, and took her head in my hands. Neither of us had ever kissed anyone before, *with tongue*, boy or girl.

"Okay, I'm gonna do it," I told her, and readied myself as if preparing for impact in a boxing match. I tilted my head and went in for the kiss. Beth opened and closed her mouth, making fake sexy moaning noises, but about two beats before our lips would have touched, she doubled over and hurled all over my shoes.

The vomiting was violent and went on for a while. When we thought it had stopped, it started again. I held her head as she vomited on the gravel road, then walked her over to the mausoleum, where she vomited again against the back wall. Tanya followed us around like a worried puppy, topless and yapping out advice. "Hold her head. She needs water. I don't got no water. You need to get her home. Throw her in the shower. Hose her off."

It took nearly an hour and a few failed attempts at keeping some Mountain Dew (sans vodka) down before Beth was in good enough shape to make the stumbling walk home, during which

I half dragged, half carried her most of the way. Somehow, we made it. It was now well into the wee hours of the night. She hit her bed and went immediately to sleep. I woke her briefly to pour water down her throat and undressed her the best I could, then curled next to her, falling quickly into a heavy sleep myself.

Her parents never even suspected. The next day, in the late afternoon, we went back to the cemetery and collected the things we'd left: our bikes, my radio, and her mother's mug. Tanya wasn't there, but her things were still as they had been the night before. I rode back to my house in the mobile home lot where I lived with my father.

He was a kind, quiet man who worked at the rock quarry full-time, and was doing his best to raise me alone, since my mother left us when I was seven. She'd always been a drunk, and when she lived with us, he did little more than cry and mumble, and they yelled at night. So when I came home from school one day and she was gone, it wasn't the worst thing. I won't say it wasn't hard, but it wasn't the worst thing. It was bad at first, not knowing where she was or if she was ever coming back, but eventually I got used to not caring, and by the time I was that age, I didn't really think about it anymore.

Dad did his best. He didn't always know quite what to say to me, but he was always good to me. When I came in that day, hungover at twelve years old in the late afternoon, he greeted me and motioned toward our dinner, which was laid out on the kitchen table. He had bought us Subway sandwiches and we ate them in the living room, watching the football game as we often did on Sunday nights, as if nothing extraordinary had happened. He had no idea. Of course, he had no reason to suspect anything was different. As far as he knew, I'd simply spent the night at my friend's house and came home the next afternoon, as I had many times before. But somehow, I thought he would be able to see it on me, this change, whatever it was, brought on by the events of the previous night. It was so obvious to me, and it didn't even register with him, I was ruined for the world. We both were, Beth and I, spoiled, in a weird way. Our safe, simple world where our basic needs were met would no longer be enough for us. We longed to taste the freedom of her lack.

It was hard for us to sleep that night. We lay awake in our separate beds, our minds racing with thoughts of her. In the space between waking and dreams, I saw her slinking in her baby blue panties and running shoes, topless up the night road, the stars guiding her on toward the truck stop where scurrilous men handed her bills to crawl up into their oily cabins and take them in her mouth. The smell of Listerine filled my nose and tickled the back of my tongue. We pondered what it was like to be her, free as her, and would she let us in again to that place where we could be free with her?

We went back as often as we could, which was quite often. After school and after our homework was complete, most days, we sat with her until sunset. She told us about things. She answered our child's questions. She answered every question we asked and told us things we never would have thought to ask. She could talk for hours on end without tiring of the conversation. She could dance to country music on her old radio, and twirl for us, and gorge herself on candy, and comb her hair straight, and smoke infinite quantities of cigarettes. I took up smoking with her as a lark, and began turning pale from the horrible menthols. Beth didn't smoke again, and didn't drink with her, either. She was afraid of it after that night of violent vomiting, but I would help myself to a shot of whiskey here and there, which I sipped as we sat, enjoying the privacy of the mausoleum walls: insulated by the bodies of the rich dead.

Soon, we sat with her after school and after we'd only pretended to do our homework, and our grades began to fall, and I became paler, and neither of us took much interest in the school, or the playground antics of our peers, or the yammerings of our parents and teachers. We had more important things to think about. We ran errands for her. We made grocery lists and bought her close approximations of the food she'd asked for at the local super-market: peanut butter and jelly, bread, Lunchables, and Go-Gurt pouches, cookies, and canned SpaghettiOs; nothing perishable, because she didn't have a refrigerator. If not for us, she would have lived off of the chips and candy bars and liquor she purchased late at night at the truck stop. She paid us for our errands, three dollars here, five dollars even, sometimes, for a big haul. She seemed to have a nearly endless supply of small bills. I had a hunch I knew what most of the cash was from, but I didn't ask. Although she was quick to divulge information about her personal life, and about the seedy goings-on of humankind, there were some things we did not ask, which I knew she would never be honest about.

It was in the paper for weeks. I noticed it one morning as I sat with my father, eating cereal, him drinking his coffee and reading the sports section, which is all he really ever read of the news-paper. The news part of the paper was lying on the table in front of me, and my eyes caught a headline: "Search Still in Progress for Woman Robber." I read the story. A woman, wearing a ski mask, weighing approximately one hundred pounds, about five feet five inches tall, had robbed a gas station in a neighboring town.

They weren't sure if she'd even had a weapon. She'd held up the place with something that could have easily been anything, shoved into a paper bag and pointed at the cashier as if it was a gun. The cashier was a kid, a girl of only sixteen, so she gave the woman everything: all the money in the register as well as in the safe, which unfortunately had not been locked, so she got away with nearly two thousand dollars in small bills. We lived in a very rural area of neighboring small towns, and this sort of incident was quite uncommon. My father noticed what I was reading. "Goddamned meth heads are everywhere lately," he grumbled, shaking his head and sipping his coffee.

There was a number to call if you had any information. Although I assumed the suspect was Tanya, I didn't even think about calling the number. It would have been a betrayal. She was ours now, Beth's and mine. She was like our pet. She was like a cat. We could leave her alone all day, sometimes even skipping days, and she would still be there, crooning and waiting to be fed and paid attention to.

We loved her. We loved her in different ways. For Beth, she was like a cool older sister, or older girlfriend. Beth felt excited and like she was doing something very taboo and very mature when she was with her. For me, it was a little different. I felt something that Beth also felt. On top of everything else, I needed to keep her well. I felt sorry for her, and I liked feeding her and caring for her. She was my friend, in a way, and I always felt like I was having an adventure when I was with her, but I also felt pity for her, hiding out alone there like she was. Nowhere to go, no one to see except the truckers and us.

Three weeks became a month and then, somehow, more than two months had passed, and winter was upon us. Tanya was becoming increasingly agitated during our visits. By the end of December, it would begin snowing, we all knew, and it wouldn't let up until February. She didn't have a plan. She never had. She mused about getting one of the truckers to let her hitch a ride with him out to California, or down to Florida. But there was something about the way she said this that let us all know these were only pipe dreams.

Beth snuck her blankets from her parents' storage, and I bought her many sweatshirts and sweatpants from the dollar store with money she'd given me, which she wore in layers. She was paranoid that the FBI was after her. Sometimes it was the CIA and sometimes it was the NSA, though it was never the local police, which is what she should have probably actually been worried about. The reasons that the FBI, or CIA, or NSA might be after her were various and confusing, having to do with her husband, or boyfriend or brother, depending on which incarnation of the story she was telling that day, having deep government connections and trying to frame her, for what, it was unclear. She simply said, a wild look in her eyes, "I know that fucker's tryin' to frame me." And after she took what she never wavered from referring to as her sinus medicine, she would lament the baby, which had either been beaten out of her, or which she'd been forced against her will to have aborted, or which she'd miscarried. I wasn't sure what Beth believed, but I knew there was no husband or boyfriend, or brother, and there was no baby. There was just her shocked mind panicking like a tormented cat lurching at some constant apparition in the corners of her consciousness.

She was wide-eyed and more and more paranoid. Her past was a perpetually shifting narrative that, as she recalled its stories, sometimes seemed to surprise even her. She had no past, or she had many pasts. She had no foreseeable future. It was getting colder, and she had no plan. She was scratching at her own flesh till it scabbed and then scratching the scabs. She was trembling and chewing her lips. Sometimes, during the last two weeks, where she was chewing was bleeding, and one day one of her teeth fell out, and Beth cried, and I knew something had to change. There was blood coming from her gums where the blackened tooth had fallen out, and sinus medicine was crusted around her nose, and she just laughed and laughed, and laughed at the whole thing, and I knew something had to change.

It was a Thursday, dangerously encroaching upon a bad winter, and we were riding our bikes from school, an activity we would soon have to forsake, due to the oncoming snows. We'd start taking the bus again, and *we* would be fine. But what would she do? She didn't have a plan, but luckily, I had one for her.

I told Beth I didn't want to go to the cemetery right away. I wanted to take a different route, down Sycamore Street, where I knew of at least two empty houses that I thought could provide a good respite from the cold. We lived in a small town of just three thousand people, tucked into a valley on the western side of a small mountain. Nothing much happened. People didn't move there. People either stayed, and stayed, or moved away, and the economy had been on a steady decline since I was small, so there was not a shortage of shabby, empty houses that had either been foreclosed on or altogether abandoned by owners who'd lost all hope of selling. The first house was in the middle of a residential block of town and quite exposed for our purposes, but we checked it out anyway. It was a small one-story thing, with a rotting porch, and many notices of condemnation stapled to the door and boarded-up windows. We crept in through the back door, and when we entered, it became obvious that we weren't the only ones who'd broken in. Cigarette butts and empty beer cans littered the stained floor, and stupid graffiti covered the living room walls. It was cold inside, and we discovered that one of the bedroom ceilings was greatly compromised, crumbling in the corner, and rotten all the way through in one section, exposing the house to the elements.

We went down the road to the second place I had in mind, which was a larger two-story home that had been empty for a year, that rested on the edge of the residential street, tucked away inside a large, fenced-in yard surrounded by shrubbery, overgrown weeds, and trees, some of which were evergreens. This, I thought, would provide good cover, and if she draped the windows with blankets, would not draw much attention during the winter, even if she burned her candles at night. Beth and I dropped our bikes on the side of the road and crawled under the fence, pushing our way through the brambly weeds. It was more difficult to get inside this house as the doors had been boarded quite securely, but we were able to jimmy a basement window, and once we were inside, we saw that the house was in very good condition: dusty but sturdy, and not at all rotten. There was even a couch in the large living room, which, although it smelled of mold, would be usable. We were surprised to find that, although there was no electricity and the gas to the stove had been cut off, the water still worked. We could flush the toilet and run the sink. It didn't get hot, but it was something. Beth was elated. "This'll be like a mansion for her," she beamed. We decided that we would convince her to move that night, after dark, but before it got too late. We went home, and I told my dad that I would be watching movies at Beth's house until evening, and she told her parents that she would be with me, so that we could stay out past our regular curfew.

We met at the cemetery at six. We were disappointed to find Tanya wasn't there. We spoke briefly about going to the truck stop to look for her, but somehow, that wasn't an option. I think that would have been too real. Somehow, she would have seemed like a different person to us in a less private context. We waited around for a good hour. The mausoleum was cold, its stone walls exacerbating the chill, serving only to keep out the gusts of wind that came up intermittently as we waited. The sun was set, and we lit candles, noting that we could see our own breath rising and falling before us inside the mausoleum like a spectral warning of what would only be getting worse.

When Tanya finally arrived, she was drunker than usual, and the residue of her sinus medicine was crusted underneath her left nostril. "Heya, girlies," she greeted us. "You're out late. You bring me something? Here, look what I got." She pulled two packets of Twinkies, some corn chips, a bag of Cheetos, a Pepsi, and a bottle of water out of her bag and laid them on the table. "You hungry? You have dinner?" She pulled a crumpled five, and three one-dollar bills out of her pocket and tucked them under a candle on the table. "I made some money today. It comes and it goes, though, don't it? That was twenty big ones, and now look at it. Dang." She'd told us she did "odd jobs" for the truckers, which Beth had presumed to mean helping them clean their trucks and pump gas, obviously not connecting the rantings of the first night of our meeting to actual, ongoing activities. At first, Tanya had been polite enough to answer Beth with, "Yeah, sure, that kinda stuff. I help 'em change the oil, give the hood a rub-down. Ha!" but she'd soon after that, during one of her sinus medicine binges, divulged and described in great detail exactly what the odd jobs looked like, and felt like, and smelled like, and how much she got paid for each type of odd job. Beth thought it was cool. I tried not to think about it too much.

She shook the Twinkie in my face. "You want some?"

I declined, but Beth opened the bag of Cheetos and ate a handful. I was anxious about getting things done, because we only had a few hours left before we had to be home.

"We found something for you," I told her. "It's a place you can live in the winter. It's warm."

"It's a big house," Beth said, chewing on the Cheetos. "You'll love it."

"What are you talkin' about? What house?" Tanya asked, tearing open the bag of Twinkies and diving right in. "These are so good," she said through the mouthful. "You know what I seen today? I seen this guy with a weird little dog with a bandanna tied around its neck that said 'little bitch,' and I said to him, 'Now hey, do you know what the difference is between a bitch and a—'"

"You've got to start packing," I interrupted her. "We can stay a little later tonight and help you move." I took a blanket off her bed and began folding it. "I can ride you on my bike on the pegs. We'll have to make a couple trips. We can put your stuff in our baskets." I finished folding one blanket, set it down on the floor and went to folding the next. But as soon as I'd picked it up, Tanya snatched it out of my hands.

"What the hell are you doin'?" she snapped. "What you got in your head? Move where? What are you talking about?"

"The house we found you!" Beth said excitedly. "It's so beautiful. And it's totally empty."

"Where's it at? How you know no one ain't coming back?"

"It's abandoned," I said. "It's all boarded up, but we've got a way in."

"Why would we go in?"

82

I rolled my eyes. "You can live there through the winter," I said loudly, exasperated.

"Where's this house at?" Tanya asked, seeming not at all pleased.

"It's in town," Beth said. "Just at the end of Sycamore, before Natural Bridge Road. It's real private." She tried, "It's hidden so no one will know you're in there."

"Hunt-uh, Hunt-uh." Tanya sat down on the bed and folded her arms across the blanket she held. She shook her head no several times. "I ain't goin' into town. They'll find me there."

"No one's looking for you anymore," I told her, deeply annoyed. "No one cares." This pissed her off.

"Naw, naw, naw." She shook her head no several more times. "I know better than that. They got radar satellites. They got infrared face recognition technology. Ain't you read the news? Huh!?" she shouted. She'd been getting more irritable and raising her voice at us for no apparent reason over the last few weeks. It was like dealing with a small child.

"But we'll go tonight. It's dark," I tried. "No one will see you."

"Oh yeah? And then what?" she snapped back. "How am I gonna live in town? How will I get to the truck stop to make my money? How will you come and see me? People'll see y'all going in and out. Then they'll know."

I hadn't thought about all of this. She had some good points, but it didn't matter. "It's too cold to stay here," I squealed. "There's going to be a blizzard next week. You've got to go."

"I don't *got* to do nothing." She tossed the blanket aside and stood, collecting her bag and taking it over to the ledge below the stained-glass Virgin Mary, where she proceeded to lay out her small mirror, onto which she dabbed her powder, which she snorted through a cut-up straw.

"We thought you'd be happy," Beth said, worry and confusion apparent in her expression.

"I appreciate what you girls tryin'a do for me," Tanya said, turning and sniffing, then taking her cigarettes out of her pocket and lighting one. She offered me one. I lit it and smoked it, cringing at the horrible menthol taste I never got used to. "But I ain't goin' into town tonight. No way. Maybe when it gets colder, if I have to. Or maybe, I'll just hitch a ride with one of those old boys out to California. Go rest my head in San Francisco. Hang out with some hippies for a while."

"You can't *stay* here anymore," I persisted. "I'm wearing a winter coat and it's freezing in here."

"It ain't *that* bad," Tanya argued. Beth came and sat down next to me dejectedly. I smoked my cigarette hard. I repeated that there was a blizzard coming soon. Beth seconded my concern. We went back and forth for a good twenty minutes, but finally we came to an agreement. We would move her on Sunday. For some reason, she thought, this would be a day when no one would be out and about to see us. I had a horrible feeling that come Sunday she would back down on her promise, but it was something, so I held onto the idea that on Sunday we'd move her, and everything would be all right, whatever all right looked like with her.

"So anyway," Tanya told us, "I said to him, 'What's the difference between a bitch and a bulldog in heat?' and he said, 'What?' And I said 'tampons,' you get it? And he looked like he was gonna turn red. And I said, 'Don't worry, hon, I don't bite . . . much.' And he laughed and laughed. They was always telling jokes like that when I was a little kid. When I was your age, there wasn't no one watching us like they watch kids now. We could do whatever and didn't have to worry about creeps like kids do now. I think it's 'cause of the video games, you know? People growing up like that . . ."

Her stories trailed on into the evening. I took a shot of whiskey and watched the clock till it was time to head home. It didn't feel the same that night as it had before. It felt like something we were quietly enduring or doing out of obligation and, somehow, on a, I suppose it would be, spiritual level, it made sense to me that the blizzard came early. Something had to change, had to move, had to freeze.

It was the very next day, a Friday, and just after lunch, we were alerted that school would be let out early. The storm was coming fast, more than three days before it was expected. I tried to sneak away when they let us out, but my dad was there waiting for me in the parking lot. The whole town was shutting down, preparing for the big blizzard. Factories were letting the workers out early, and the stores were closing. I asked my dad if I could bike home, but he was insistent, and tossed my bike in his truck bed, telling me we had to go get groceries before the store closed, because we might be snowed in for a couple of days. I saw Beth across the parking lot, getting into her mother's car, her eyes met mine for a moment, and they were wide with worry. She shook her head no at me before her mom pulled away.

All the way to the grocery store, I begged to go to Beth's house for the night. "You're not going anywhere. You could be stuck there for days." He was annoyed and emphatic. "Absolutely not." He seldom put his foot down with me, but when he did, I knew it was no use arguing.

I called Beth as soon as I got home and she was inconsolable. She kept quietly weeping. I could almost see her wiping her tears away as she repeated, "What are we going to do, Gillian? We have to do something."

"Don't worry," I told her. "She'll be okay. She's tough." But something in me knew that probably wasn't true. She was high and drunk and tweaked out most of the time, and the stone walls were more cold than she might even realize. Would she strip naked and run screaming through the onslaught? Would she drink herself into a warm slumber, her body insulated by a whiskey buzz inside a nest of blankets and confusion? I could hope. I could only hope.

The blizzard began just after eight. I watched the snow come down while my father sat on the couch, half watching television and half telling me about his day. I watched the snow come down, at first begging it to be light, then, as the wind began to pick up, I watched the blizzard like it was a murderer descending around us. I wanted to cry, but I couldn't. I wanted to tell my father, but I couldn't. This existed far from him. This existed far outside of any world I could think of as real, with laws and reason. The wind was horribly loud, hissing like a cold kettle and etching frost on the windows. The snow was phantom white, its edges sometimes blue in the streetlights, falling in morbid sheets; like those laid across faces, covering blank eyes, or pulled down for shock.

After the first hour, sleet came with the snow and rattled against the roof, and the wind shook the house where I sat, warm and safe with my father and some fake reality show going on and on, and the temperature outside steadily dropping like a regrettable stone dropped down some dark, long-forgotten well, so deep you don't hear it touch bottom and it makes you frightened of what it would be like if your own body was that stone, falling down that well of endless coldness, alone in the night.

The storm kept on through the night, and my dad told me to

go to bed, but when he finally paid full attention to me, he could see that my face was pale and my eyes crazed with worry and I was trembling all over. He put his arm around me and told me not to be scared of the storm, and I finally burst out crying, and he held me, but I couldn't stop. I was hiccuping and snorting like a baby, so he took me, for the first time since I was a baby, to bed with him, and fell asleep next to me in his work clothes, my head resting on his shoulder, while I looked out the window through tear-drenched eyes at the unrelenting night sky.

She was like our pet, and like with the pets of children, we couldn't bear to look. We trudged through the several feet of snow, packed tight in the snowsuits our parents had dressed us in before they allowed us to brave the cold only two days after the blizzard had subsided enough that the roads were passable, and it was possible to drop me off at Beth's house. We walked silently in our rubber snow boots up the road that led to the cemetery, then through the thick snow that covered the graveyard. The northmost side of the mausoleum had a snowdrift the wind had carved against it nearly five feet high. The door was cracked open, just a half inch, barely noticeable, but enough that I could tell the elements had gotten inside, and my breath also froze in the air. I placed my hand on the door and looked at my feet. I couldn't bring myself to open it. "Tanya," I said meekly. "Are you in there? Are you okay?" I closed my eyes and pressed my ear to the door's small opening, waiting for an answer. There was none. "Tanya!" Beth cried louder. "It's us! Hello! Hello!" Beth sounded like a sad little bird. I banged on the door with my gloved fist. It made a deep thudding sound against the door. Tears fell from Beth's eyes and rolled down her cheeks. They were cold and she wiped them away. "Maybe she hitched a ride to California," she said sadly. "Maybe she's at the truck stop."

I nodded yes. "She probably did. That's what she said she was going to do." We stared at the door. We didn't dare open it. Finally, I pushed it all the way closed and took the heavy chain, which still hung open dangling from the latch, and strung it through the metal hook on the wall, then looped the chain in a knot. I tugged on the door. The chain held tight. "There," I told Beth. "This way if she does come back, her place will be safe."

Beth nodded. "That's nice," she said. "I hope she does. I'll miss her." More tears streamed down her pink cheeks and she wiped them away with her thick mittens. "California is really far away." I nodded in agreement. It sure was.

We never went back to the cemetery. Of course, when we passed it on our bikes and in our parents' cars, we couldn't help but think of her, there in the mausoleum with her crumpled bills and endless cigarettes, our first taste of liquor and of freedom, real freedom we found there where we always used to go, back when the dead left us alone.

TAKE THE WAY HOME THAT LEADS BACK TO SULLIVAN STREET

"Zyprexaolanzapinezydiswithfluoxetincsymbyaxothan." She pronounced this word with familiar ease. "This drug was recalled from the pharmaceutical market, but I still have a renewable prescription. The doctor said it works best for me, regardless of the side effects."

Why are smart people always so fucking crazy? Or maybe it's not that smart people are crazy, it's just that crazy people present themselves as being super-duper smart. She did. She clung to the notion of her genius like her life depended on it. But you know, if I pull it apart, nothing she ever said was really that smart.

"Geniuses are always considered a little crazy by their generation," she told me. She told me she had a photographic memory, then she recited the names of the presidents in alphabetical order, then in the order of their presidencies. Then she did the same with the names of philosophers from Aristotle to Žižek.

But that's not really genius, is it? That's just memorizing needless shit, which I now know she probably does to keep herself from picking her toenails down till they bleed or shaving all the hair off her entire body for the third time in one day. She told me she can feel it growing.

Kali also told me she has two alternate personalities: a man whose name she doesn't know, and he is very shy, and a woman named Rose, who is a very horrible person, who slugged her first boyfriend in the face once. But she never remembers anything Rose does.

She said when she becomes these other, more horrible people, it's like a door closes in front of her and she can sometimes peek though the keyhole and see the blurred images of Rose doing things to people she knows, and she hears the muffled noises from outside, but she can't quite make out anything clearly, and she certainly can't control anything they (she) do(es).

She told me she was terrified of worms, and that at night she had dreams that copper worms were eating their way through her skin. That's why, Kali said, she could never make it through *Dune*—because of the worms. I said that probably wasn't the only reason.

Kali told me she could talk to turtles and smell architecture. She tried to make me register Libertarian. She told me she had a *feeling* about me. The first time we made love, she told me that a blinking red light named Alganon had been visiting her in the night. Alganon blinked to her from the upper corners of the bedroom as a means of communication. Alganon said that I should move in with her.

It's not like no one told me to stay away from her. Everyone who knew her, and come to think of it, even my friends upon first meeting her, told me I should run as fast as I could in the opposite direction. But Kali knew this would happen. She'd warned me.

"People don't like me," she told me. "People think I'm crazy."

"Are you?"

I guess her eyes were always a little dilated and her mouth was always smiling, especially when she was upset. She was thinner than a skeleton and cold. I don't know what that feeling was that I had for her. Was it love? Was I just mesmerized? Maybe I wanted to save her from something. Or maybe, most likely, I, like everyone else who let themselves get close to her, believed her insanity was some kind of genius. Her family sure did. They all thought of themselves as geniuses. I guess that's a big part of why it was so important to her. I guess that's why her whole identity depended on it.

Jesus. Now I'm picking *my* nails. My bags are all packed in the backseat. She didn't hear me leave, I don't think. It's three in the morning. I'm just driving around East St. Louis, aimlessly. There's a line of whores waving at me from the side of the road. They all have really impressive jewelry that glints in my headlights as I pass. I'm just sort of circling this strip. It's disgusting. There's like a little mini-mall of peep shows and porn stores and strip clubs I keep passing, right before or after I get to the whores, depending on my direction. The peep-show mini-mall wouldn't be so bad, if it weren't placed directly beside what is obviously a grade school, which shares a playground with the parking lot of the sex strip mall.

I guess I could go live in my dorm. I can't go there tonight, though. It's late and my roommate is scared enough of me as it is, even though she's only met me four times.

I have a dorm at a university in Southern Illinois. It's part of my package. I haven't even spent one night in it. I got this college package before I met Kali, when my family was still going to help me pay. They already knew I was a dyke. But when I put a face on it, *her* face anyway, they stopped helping me pay for anything. Not that they had it to give at all, anyhow. So now I have this stupid dorm I never used that I probably won't ever be able to pay for, or that I'll be paying for forever. God. Just crossing the river from St. Louis to Illinois: East St. Louis, what a shithole. And she's still there, freaking out in our fancy apartment in the West End, the one I lived in but never paid for.

Funny, I'm paying for the crappy dorm I never lived in and not paying for the fancy place I've actually been living in for the past year. I should have known, when she asked me to move in with her and I told her I couldn't afford it because of college and the dorm and all, and she said, "Don't worry about the rent," I should have known she needed me too much. Why else would a rich, straight girl overlook the three major facts that (a) I'm a dyke, (b) I'm poor as hell, and (c) I have a small drug problem?

Her parents have lots of money and a fancy house in the city, and she has a fancy apartment in a neighborhood too hip for her. Her mother is a failed actress with stock in Walmart and a permanent glass of red wine attached to her right hand. She's the spitting image of Shirley MacLaine.

When her mother met me, she asked me if anyone had ever told me that I was also the spitting image of Shirley MacLaine; a young Shirley MacLaine. I said yes, that I had heard that a lot.

She said, "Oh yes, well, women always seek out women like their mothers. Isn't that what they say? Or is it something *else* they say?" She asked me this with a resentful grin blooming on her face and a sarcastic lilt in her voice. She's a little passive-aggressive about her daughter's newfound lesbianism.

The first time I met her parents, they were hosting a Mensa party in their home. Mensa is a club for people with high IQs. They take a test, pay a due, and then hang around upper-middle-class dinner parties with a bunch of academic liberals who have no social skills. It's great.

Her mother and father are both members of Mensa. The first time I came to one of their dinner parties, I found fifteen middle-aged frumpies sitting in a circle passing around a helium balloon and reciting dirty limericks in high-pitched voices. *Ahh-ha!* I thought. *This is why she's terrified of worms and drinks soap.*

When we moved in together, she told me two things. One: she told me there was a headless woman in our kitchen who paced back and forth swinging her own head by its hair (which she always sees in kitchens, but only ever in kitchens), and Two: she told me she didn't want to take her medication anymore because she didn't need it. "I probably just needed to come out as a lesbian," she told me. "Denying that big of a part of yourself can cause serious problems," she told me.

For a while, I thought maybe she was right. When she stopped taking her medication, at first she seemed better. She didn't men-tion the headless woman again. She didn't vomit in the mornings. She stopped shaving every day. She even started talking to people her own age, making some friends at her college and hanging out in the radio station after classes. For a while there, yeah, when we went out, I enjoyed having fairly normal conversations that didn't involve detailed global statistics, the sniffing of old buildings, or cryptic discussions of the possible repercussions of her having been named after an ancient god.

Maybe, I thought, the medication *was* the problem after all. But something did bother me about the fact of her diagnosis. I hadn't really ever heard anyone complaining that schizophrenia was an overdiagnosed disorder. And there were still moments, even during those peaceful times, I noticed her staring intently at nothing, moving her lips softly, or squeezing her wrist till it bruised. Once, I asked her if she was really feeling more mentally stable, or if she was still seeing and hearing things, but trying to hide it. She snapped out of it, held my hand too hard and explained to me that this (I) was her first real relationship, and she wasn't going to fuck it up. She wasn't going to let me get away by being crazy. She didn't want me to get away at all. She never wanted me to go anywhere actually, and if I did, not without her.

My sort of unyielding urge for danger was probably what attracted me to her in the first place. Our codependent, peaceful life wasn't enough excitement for me. After five months of living with her in close-quarter domesticity, I started going out with my friends again. I think it was spurred by the big Y2K party. Everyone was sure it was going to be the end of the world. So we all totally obliterated ourselves. It felt like the end of the world that night. But other than everybody getting obliterated, nothing happened.

I took massive amounts of hallucinogens, stayed out partying until the sun came up, and returned home smelling like Vicks VapoRub. She hated it. She wanted me with her all the time. She said she didn't understand why I wanted to go to parties with my dumb friends, who, incidentally, think she's too dorky for words. And she thinks they are not intelligent enough to have the privilege of my presence.

That's the other thing she started doing when she stopped taking her medication, obsessing over calculable intelligence levels, namely, her IQ. She'd been dragging me to at least one Mensa dinner a week, most of which are held at her parents' house. She started threatening to take the Mensa entrance test a few weeks ago. But then, she ruminated that she didn't need to take the test because she's already an unofficial member. The truth is, she was terrified to take the test . . . terrified she might fail. Everyone just assumes she is an out-of-the-ballpark genius. Her parents excuse her schizophrenic tendencies, which mostly show up as small moments of quirky darkness or anxiety in their presence, as side effects of her genius. If she took the test and failed, her insanity would no longer be viewed as the residue of a great mind at work, but just what it was—crazy for the sake of crazy. And I knew being exposed in this way would totally unhinge her.

I never encouraged her one way or another. She could take the stupid test or not. I openly found the whole idea completely dull.

Earlier today, Kali asked me to go to a Mensa party with her, but I had other plans.

"Please," she begged. "It'll be different this time. It's gonna be wild."

"It's never been *wild*, honey, come on. The wildest it's ever gotten was when they decided to play strip Trivial Pursuit, and that was really just kind of uncomfortable."

"No," she said, "I promise, it's gonna be wild. The guy at the radio station gave me something. I've been saving it for tonight."

"What did he give you?"

"It's a surprise. I've been saving it for tonight. Please. Just this once? I promise you, this *thing* he gave me will make the conversations much more interesting."

I guess she thought she needed to make her life more interesting to me in order to keep me in it. I was sure she had some coke or maybe pot or something, trying to lure me away from my drugged-up friends by becoming my drugged-up girlfriend. But hey, it worked. I thought it might be kinda funny to interact with the Mensans high. So I went with her.

I grabbed a hitter and a mirror just in case Kali didn't have the foresight, and we drove to her parents' house.

The party was already under way when we pulled up. A few of the Mensans were still filing into the small, near-mansion, colonial-style house, which she said smelled like grapes (colonial architecture, that is). The lights were all lit up and I could hear the sound of drinking songs coming from the living room. They were singing, "A ghost that's meshugenah makes Mendelssohn go drown."

She turned to me and held out her tiny closed fist. "You ready?"

"I brought a mirror, and a hitter," I told her. "Which is it?"

She opened her hand. Sitting in her palm was a small, folded piece of tinfoil.

"Oh my god, you're not serious."

She opened the tinfoil. Inside were two little stamps bearing images of the pink elephants from *Dumbo*, which smiled up at me.

"Acid? You want to do acid at your parents' dinner party?"

She smiled excitedly at me. "Yeah. What? You've done it before, haven't you?"

"Yeah, I've done it a lot. Enough to know you shouldn't do it at your parents' dinner party."

"Oh, but cocaine would have been all right?"

"Yeah, somehow, it *would*. I mean, it's very different. Have you ever even done acid?"

"Yeah, I did it once. It wasn't intense. It didn't really even have any effect on me. Everyone else was tripping but, I don't know, I have a high alcohol tolerance. Maybe I just have a high tolerance in general."

"For acid? An acid tolerance?"

"Yeah. It had virtually no effect on me. Everything was just black and white for five hours. But other than that, I felt totally normal."

"Mmmm-hhhhmmm."

"Listen, we don't have to stay the whole time. If it gets too weird, we can go for a walk or just go upstairs and hang alone."

We put the little papers on our tongues and let them dissolve. I wanted to stay outside for a while, smoke a couple cigarettes and prepare myself. But in the time it took to "prepare myself," the acid started kicking in. And I realized, as I always do the first ten minutes of a trip, that there is no way to prepare oneself for tripping. You can tell yourself all sorts of dumb shit like, *Just keep quiet and no one will know*. Or, *use the drug, don't let it use you . . .* la-di-da. But acid always surprises you. It always comes up with something you had no way to prepare yourself for. My friend Rob swore acid never got the better of him, swore to all sorts of meditation techniques that helped him get the most out of his trips, "to control it," he said. Why, then, did his mother find him barreling naked through a cornfield on all fours, the words JESUS CHRIST WHY? written backward on his forehead in red lipstick?

Because there is no way to foresee that these sorts of things might happen. And if there is, how can the before-acid-you tell the post-acid-you not to do these things, no matter how much you want to? How can you foresee that you might *want* to strip naked and etch the words JESUS CHRIST WHY? backward on your forehead in red lipstick? How can you control that kind of insane wanting? There's no way to explain this, really. Let's just say, there is no way you can prepare not to react to self-inflicted schizophrenia.

Self-inflicted schizophrenia. That's what tripping is. I never saw it so clearly before that night. But seeing it as such brought up in me a big question, which I probably don't really want to know the answer to: What is insanity?

When we walked into her parents' house, everything was normal. And that's what I kept telling myself, *This is normal, and this feels normal. I'm still acting normal.*

Jan, her mom, came up, handed me a glass of wine, and kissed me on both cheeks. "That's normal."

"What's normal?"

Fuck did I say that out loud?

"It's normal . . . in Europe, to double-kiss like that," I told her.

"Mmm. You're so worldly, aren't you?" She never missed a chance to make me feel dumb. "Come in here then. There's something I want to show you. I think you're really going to be intrigued by this. You just can't believe it."

The way she said it, I thought she might be leading me into a secret laboratory, and perhaps we would find Dr. Strangelove sitting there with the red button. Whatever it was, it seemed very important the way she kept turning to me and nodding, saying, "Yes, yes, it's coming any minute now," and smiling with pride and anticipation. "I've got this really terrific *thing*, you just *have* to see it. And tell me what you think. Don't be afraid to give me your real opinion," she said, an eerie, almost ravenous smile spreading across her face.

All this anticipation culminated in her taking me into the den and showing me an antique lampshade.

She talked for literally ten minutes about the history of the lampshade, the design, where she bought it, who owned it before her, and why it was a relevant historical piece. Rich people are hard enough to deal with not on acid. The things that excite them are confusing and hilarious enough without a psychedelic lens magnifying everything. As she went on about the lampshade, I was biting the inside of my cheek very hard to keep from laughing, and I suddenly realized I'd bitten it too hard and I could taste blood in my mouth. My eyes opened up very wide and I said, "Oh!" She thought I was pleased, so she moved on to the cabinet the lamp was sitting on. At this point I became worried that my feet might be melting.

"This, on the other hand, is not actually an antique," she said of the cabinet.

I made some sort of very surprised expression, because I had just relearned how to cross my toes.

"I know," she said. "It's amazing! Jerry made this. He just finished it yesterday. I didn't know my husband was such a wonder with wood. He stained it this way and la-di-da, and the cut is intended to represent designs from the something-something era." (I wasn't totally listening.) "And do you know what we're going to do?" I stared at the cabinet blankly. "We're throwing a birthday party for the cabinet." She laughed gleefully at herself. "We're having a birthday party for it next week!" she repeated.

"I'm sorry."

She took this as if it were a question: a request for an explanation. But it was very simply an expression of the deep and pressing sorrow I felt for her at that moment.

"A cabinet birthday party!" Liz boomed, suddenly beside me. Liz was a soft-spoken poetic type who always had to wear something purple. Even if it was "just a dash," she never, and I mean never, left the house without at least a bit of purple. She was a rich, pseudo-hippie, Buddhist, Jewish journalist. She possessed all of the categories that, at least one of which, most people at the party fit into. "A cabinet party for the cabinet!" she squealed, excitedly, clapping her hands. "I'm wearing my new purple dress." She was so excited, her oversized tits were shaking beneath her purple sweatshirt. I stared too long at them.

"Are you coming?"

"No!" I said, too forcefully.

"Why not? Do you have other plans?"

"I don't know what my plans are," I said, anger showing in my voice. "But I'm not coming."

I usually had an all right time at the parties, but I never felt a connection with these people like my girlfriend did. Mostly I just drank wine and made sarcastic comments when they hurled their trivia disguised as conversation at me. They seemed to like me, though. They were always sort of awed by the fact that I have no interest in appearing super smart, and I can't quote statistics, but I can quote Skunk Anansie, Warhol, Bill Hicks, and Jello Biafra. My clothes always fit me, and I do my hair before I leave the house. I am the cool kid come down among them.

It always gets tired for the cool kid, though. Tonight, I worried my sarcastic comments might soon become too close to just being out-and-out malicious. This sudden burst of irrational anger startled Jan and Liz, probably even more than the time I freaked out on Walter, the linguist pedophile who showered his undying affection on me until I turned nineteen.

He'd given me a piece of manganese with the word "Manganese" inscribed on it from his actual elemental table. That's right, he kept a real elemental table in his house. It took up an entire room, the table laid out as a vinyl print on the floor and actual samples of all of the elements in the appropriate place, with the exception, of course, of a few radioactive ones. It was rumored, though, that he had two of the minorly radioactive elements locked in a safe by the dresser. He'd cornered me at every party for three months (during the time I was only just eighteen), attempting to deconstruct the origin of my strange name. He'd begun invoking some sexually explicit phrases from Africa, and I finally told him, in so many words, to go fuck himself, loudly. Speak of the devil.

There was a tap on my shoulder. It was Walter; the sixty-two-year-old self-admitted pedophile with a PhD in linguistics. It's not like he's constantly proclaiming his pedophilia. He just lets it slip from time to time toward the end of some of the more drunken dinner parties. He has no children of his own and has placed a swing set in his backyard for the neighbor kids. He justifies this action by saying he never actually interacts with the neighbor children, he just watches while they swing. So no one gets hurt. It's a win-win. After he lets shit like this slip, he always finds some "clever" way to remind everyone that he has a PhD in linguistics, like it's okay to be a pedophile as long as you are very smart.

"What's that joke you told me last time?" he asked me, pinching the end of his greasy gray beard. "Ladies," he said, motioning for the two other women to pay attention, "she told me this amazing joke last time, did you hear it? It goes, *A Buddhist walks up to a hot dog vendor and says, 'Give me one with everything on it.'*"

The ladies looked very contemplatively at him and, I suppose, because he had a PhD in linguistics, they were wondering if perhaps it was just that his joke was over their heads and he was very smart, or if it was that I was very dumb and he was just being nice by retelling my ignorant joke.

He seems like a really skilled pedophile compared to his skills in linguistics. The joke was supposed to go, *A Buddhist walks up to a hot dog vendor and says, "Make me one with everything."*

I tried to correct him, but the walls were melting, as were my feet. I shook my head slowly, no. It took me several long seconds to force out the words, "Make me one with everything," slowly . . . loudly . . . meaningfully. And I am not sure anyone connected my statement with the joke Walter had just told incorrectly, or if my statement existed autonomously, in their minds, from that conversation. "Make me one with everything," a desperate plea I was suddenly lobbing at them. Jan raised an eyebrow at me, and nodded.

There was the sound of an elephant honking from the other room. I jumped. Jan and Liz made disgusted faces. "Why do we invite him?" Liz whispered to Jan.

"He's a chapter member," Jan said in a singsong tone, throwing up the hand that was not attached to the wineglass, as if to say she had no power over the situation.

The sound of the elephant booming had come from Ed. He was

an obese math wiz with Coke-bottle glasses who had recently been fired for excessive flatulence from his job in military intelligence.

"I swear to god, if he eats all of my penguin hors d'oeuvres, I'm going to kill him." He'd also once been kicked out of an all-you-can-eat buffet for pulling his chair right up to the buffet and eating directly out of the food bins.

Jan tugged on my shoulder. "Have you seen the penguin olives?" I shook my head no. She led me excitedly out of the den and into the dining room where a statue of Bacchus laughed down at the table, joyfully watching over the impressive spread of cheeses, mini-sandwiches, and fruit. Kali came up beside me and took hold of my arm. Her eyes were wide and she was smiling an oversized smile. She was also sweating. Her mom asked if she was feeling all right. She replied too happily that she was a little nauseous, but it was probably just the medication. (She hadn't told her mother she'd stopped taking her medication nearly a year ago.)

Jan ran her finger around the rim of her glass and swayed her hips proudly. "These took me hours to make, but I did it myself. Have you ever seen anything like this?" she asked, holding up an olive that had been cut to resemble a tiny penguin. "I just cut the stomach out and made it the head. It's stuck on with a toothpick, see. Then I stuffed the stomach with cream cheese. The beak is a carrot, and the little wings are easy to make, just two slits in the sides." The penguin was flapping its wings and waddling in her hand. It squawked at me. My stomach turned queasy. "Here," she said, "try it."

"I'm a vegetarian," I told her.

"Oh, it's not really a penguin! Don't be silly!" Then she grabbed the bottom of my chin and literally shoved the penguin hors d'oeuvres in my mouth. "I spent nearly three hours making these," she told me as she shoved it in. "You have to try it."

I closed my mouth and tried to chew while she watched with near reverie, but I could feel the oily flesh of the penguin struggling against my tongue. I heard the miniature penguin squealing and squawking in there. It was too much, I opened my mouth and spit it out into my hand, the black-and-white muck of it just lay there, immobile. Jan let out a long disgusted "Ewwwee," and backed slowly away from me.

My girlfriend started laughing uncontrollably as I dumped the remains of the dead penguin into the trash can. "Sorry," I told Jan. But she just shook her head at me and left the room. This wasn't going well.

My girlfriend took my arm. "It's okay. Let's go sit with them."

I protested but she pulled me in. We sat on the couch with Liz, across from Walter and Jerry, my girlfriend's father, and some others. "So, when are you going to take the test?" Liz asked, patting her on the knee.

A look of horror struck her face. She looked to me for some answer, pulled her shoulders up and down, and let out a long sigh. "I've been thinking about it, and I think I'm not taking it," she said. "I probably wouldn't pass anyway, and I'm fine being an unofficial member of Mensa. You guys are my family, anyway. You're my best friends."

I scanned the room, Ed, Walter, Liz, her father, and two frumpies in the corner playing chess, only taking a swig of their gin and tonic when they lost a piece, and something in my stomach flipped.

These were her parents' best friends.

These were *her* best friends.

These were the people who saw her most and never see her at all.

These people were all at least twenty years older than her.

These were the only people she wasn't terrified of.

Except for me.

I was her lover.

I was the only peer she ever interacted with on any intimate level.

"Nonsense. You would pass! You are so obviously smart. Gee, just becoming a lesbian . . ." she motioned to me and winked. "To hell with men. That's just smart," Liz said.

"That *is* smart," one of the frumpy hippie-dippies told her.

"I wish I had thought of it, don't you, Jan?" Liz asked Kali's mother, who'd come to stand in the doorway. Jan took a big gulp of wine and nodded with a passive-aggressive, not really, but really kinda homophobic, "liberal" clench-toothed smile.

"I don't feel well," Kali told them. "It's the medication. It's giving me a headache."

"Well, you do look a little clammy," her mother told her.

It had been about thirty minutes since we took the acid. We were just getting to the top of our climb. We both desperately needed to get away from them. Everything was getting too meaningful, and for me at least, it was still also melting. We excused ourselves to go upstairs.

In the guest bedroom I immediately got very caught up by a piece of rogue taxidermy mounted on the wall—a deer head with a red bulb in place of its nose. "Rudolph," they always joked, "a small-game prize from Christmas Eve, 1976." I sat on the edge of the bed, wavering and pondering the fate of dead things.

She sat next to me with her hand on my knee. I thought she

was staring into my ear, but she was probably trying to get me to look her in the eye.

"Could you imagine," I asked, "if someone made a joke of your dead body like this?"

"I can't imagine, 'cause I wouldn't know. I'd be dead. Anyway, who's to say that gravestones and mausoleums aren't funny?"

I looked into her eyes. They were dilated and shining, almost completely black.

"Think about it," she said. "It's kind of hilarious."

We sat there thinking about the hilarity of gravestones and mausoleums.

"All the giant gray angels."

"The Taj Mahal."

"The Louvre."

"The Pyramids."

"The Pyramids." We took up with a laughing fit that sent us into tears and collapsed us on the bed.

"You know," she said, "I was named after an ancient god of destruction?"

I laughed harder. "Oh no, really? You've *never* mentioned it. Not once. Not every other day."

I was on my back, holding my stomach because it hurt from laughing.

Her laughing had settled. She rolled over on top of me and bit at my neck. She whispered in my ear in a voice that did not differentiate between malice and seduction.

"You know, the French call orgasms 'a little death.' Why don't people build monuments to really good orgasms?"

She grabbed my nipples with her thin fingers and twisted. All of her touches felt distant and abstract. I thought she could twist my nipples off and it wouldn't matter. It would just be my body. Maybe it would even look pretty, my little pink nipple resting hard in the palm of her hand. I grabbed at her wrist and held her hand up to my face, inspecting it. Was there a nipple there in her palm? I saw it for a second, but then it disappeared. She rubbed my forehead. I was sweating.

"Are you tripping hard, baby?"

"Yeah. Aren't you?"

"I don't know." She wiped the sweat off her forehead. "Maybe I can't tell the difference. I just know I want you really badly." She sucked her fingers and pushed her hand down the front of my pants. Then she pinched my clit between her thumb and finger and tugged at it with little tugs. "You like that?" she asked.

I nodded yes. I did like it, but not in the way I usually did. I liked the thought of it—the image it put in my head—a little pink pebble between two little fleshy things. It looked like a Dalí painting. We were moving, and I was on a ship traveling to Egypt. I was a slave lying on my back at the bottom of the boat, and there was an Egyptian god in the shadows of the ceiling laughing at me.

She had gotten us both undressed somehow, and was pulling me under the covers. I felt like I was sinking below the waves. It was all happening to me. I wasn't doing it. There was wetness in my ears, her tongue, and something moving inside me to the motion of waves. I felt suddenly panicked and out of control. I looked to the shadow god on the ceiling. It spoke. *You have free will*, the Egyptian god told me. *Become . . . become.*

I grabbed her hips and flipped her on her back, placing myself on top. We stared into each other's dilated pupils. She slipped one leg between mine and the other around my hip. My clit was sliding against hers and she was moaning. I fucked her like that for a few minutes, but again, it didn't necessarily feel sexual or even physical. I just saw it. I saw our two cunts together sliding and pushing. They looked like two flowers smashed together on a rainy sidewalk. Hers was swollen. Mine was flat. It wasn't hot. It was just kind of sad and pretty.

Then I got the thought that it didn't matter what I was feeling. That this was something I had begun, and I had to finish it, like a monument. My purpose was to make her come.

I put two fingers inside and circled her walls methodically. She was shaking and tears were coming from her eyes. *Good*, I thought. *It's working.*

I sat up and she raised herself halfway to my mouth. I bowed down and let my tongue go fast as I could, keeping my fingers pumping inside her, my tongue like a little paddleboat engine against her tip. She got very wet till it was dripping down my wrist, which felt very strange. She smashed herself against my face. This move completely overwhelmed me.

It was as if a giant pink butterfly had landed in my mouth and was beating its wings frantically against my face. But it wasn't just as if that were happening. I was tripping. It was happening. Its little bug body was in my mouth. Its giant wings were beating my face. It was a sort of terrifying ecstasy. *This must be the beginning*, I thought. *We are beginning to change, "to become."*

The thing about acid is, your perception of what you're doing and what you are actually doing are often two very different things. I thought I was kneeling in a field with my hand inside a plump yellow melon, a frantic butterfly in my mouth, and an Egyptian god watching over me.

I was actually kneeling on the floor in front of her parents' guest bed, motionless for the past minute, with my motionless fingers in my girlfriend, whose cunt was in my open, motionless mouth, and I had apparently begun humming in one loud steady "Ohmmm" tone. In short, she had kept having sex and I had begun meditating.

"What the hell are you doing?" She pulled away from me and sat up.

I opened my eyes. We were still in her parents' guest bedroom. I shook my head and let it drop into my hands. She came over and held me. "Are you okay, baby? What's going on? What are you thinking? What did you feel? You can tell me."

I tried to explain the haze. "I just thought," I told her, "that if I made you come, you would turn into something. You know, whatever you really are, what best represents you. Like a monument."

Her face grew cold, grave. "And what exactly did you think I would turn into?"

"I don't know."

"Tell me," she insisted very intently.

"I guess I thought you would sprout wings or something. You know . . . like a gargoyle, or like . . ." I searched for words, "a demon."

"A demon?" she squealed, angry and accusatory.

"That's not what I meant. No, never mind. Wrong choice."

She stood and started pacing. "So you think you know everything now, huh?"

"What are you talking about? Just calm down."

"You think you know what I really am?"

"Aw, come on. I didn't mean demon, *exactly*. I mean, I guess it kind of is—"

"What else did it tell you?" she shouted.

"What else did what tell me?"

"What else did *he* tell you?"

"Who?"

She pointed to the ceiling. "Him." Then she said some Egyptian name I don't remember and my hairs jumped off my body.

The Egyptian god on the ceiling was *my* hallucination. I hadn't shared it with her. I stared up at the Egyptian god and she stared at him too. We both saw him there, hovering above us, growling through angry brick teeth with a face that kept turning to sand and reconstructing itself. It's very off-putting to share the same hallucination with someone. It makes you wonder whether it's really a hallucination.

"This is getting too crazy," I said, collecting my clothes. I didn't dare make eye contact with her. I just headed to the bathroom and locked myself in. It probably took me twenty minutes to get dressed. I splashed some water on my face and checked to see if I looked presentable. But there was really no way to tell, the way my face kept shifting and changing color like that. How long had we been up here? An hour? It felt like about an hour.

When I came out, she was seated in a chair in the hallway. She must have been waiting for me, but she didn't turn when I came out. She just stared straight ahead at the wall, keeping her hands folded in her lap and her back upright, ridged, like she was in a trance. But she was whispering to something. I knelt beside her. "Baby, it's gonna be all right. You just need to act fairly normal for the next ten minutes. We're gonna get out of here and take a little walk. We'll come down in a couple hours. Then we can go and eat cheese sandwiches."

She stopped whispering to whatever it was and tuned her head mechanically to face me. Her eyebrows twisted into a point reminiscent of Joan Crawford as she intoned, "Cheese sandwiches? Cheese sandwiches!!!" like these two words together created the most hateful and absurd of concoctions.

"All right. Here we go." I lifted her by the shoulders, keeping my grip on her as we headed down the stairs. We'd have to pass through the kitchen, the dining room, and the hall before we were out. We'd also have to say goodbye to her mother, and for her part at least, I could blame any strange behavior on the medication her mother did not know she'd stopped taking. I was getting it all planned out. It seemed doable.

We reached the bottom of the stairs. As we turned into the kitchen I felt her tiny arm begin to tremble under my grip. She set her pointed gaze at the far corner of the room.

"You see her?" she whispered.

But I tried to ignore her inquiry. "Just in one door, out the other, babe. Just say bye-bye to mom, and here we go."

She turned on me, tearing her arm loose from my clutch. "I'm not fucking tripping!" she said, sort of stage-whispering, like a whispering scream. "I have to live with this every day. Now you're in *my* world, apparently. You can see it too, so *try*. She's right there!" She pointed to the corner.

I knew who she was talking about, the headless woman she always saw in kitchens. I glanced over quickly. Maybe I could have seen her too if I'd tried, but I really, really didn't want to. I shook my head no. "No, I don't see anything."

She tapped my arm. "She's coming over here. She sees me too. Oh god. She's never looked at me before."

"How can she be looking at you if she doesn't have a head?"

"She's *carrying* her head!" she snapped, as if it were obvious.

"Honey, this is just a bad fucking trip. Calm down. Remember what I told you. Use the drug, don't let it use you."

"Don't give me that raver shit. The headless woman can see me. This is fucking serious." She grabbed her chest and gasped.

"What?"

"She's right here in front of us, next to you. She's talking."

At this point there was nothing I could do but watch her listen. I was absolutely tripping hard myself, but trying not to show it. I had my own problems, like the way the yellowish kitchen light was sliding down the walls and dripping from the cracks in the paint, and, as always, my melting feet.

I guess I must have been pretty distracted by this sort of stuff, 'cause when I started paying attention again, my girlfriend was holding a butcher knife.

There's nothing like the sight of a person on acid holding a foot-long knife that brings you that sobering feeling one so often longs for just after their peak.

I swear to god, I flew four feet to the opposite door, away from her. She was holding the knife up by her head like she was Elmer Fudd hunting rabbits.

"Honey, whatcha doing?"

She didn't look at me. "She put her head back on her neck," she told me. "She wants me to cut it off again, or wait, no, she's shaking her head no. What's that? What?"

"No, honey. Don't cut it off again. Just leave it on. That's the nice thing to do," I tried.

"No, no. She's speaking."

"What's she saying?"

She turned her black eyes to me and smiled like she was one of those women on a cooking show and she was about to show me how to bake a cake . . . made out of children. "She wants me to cut off someone else's head," she told me.

I took another step back, literally straddling the doorframe, ready to bolt. "You fucking ignore her, do you understand me?"

She tilted her head like she was trying.

"Good," I continued. "Now one of two things is going to happen: either you are going to put down the knife, or you're not going to put down the knife, but I'm gonna leave you alone here with your mom and your headless friend, and you are never, do you understand me, NEVER going to see me *ever* again." That was the best I could do.

She stood there pondering her options.

"You have three seconds to put it down or I (pause) am (pause) gone (pause) *forever!*"

She looked from me to the headless woman.

"One."

She shook her head no in the direction of the headless woman.

"Two."

She tilted her head at me again, like a puppy, and nodded.

"Two and a half."

She laid the knife on the counter.

"Walk over here, slowly. Don't look at her."

She came over slowly like she was walking a tightrope. When she was finally within my reach, I grabbed her, tugged her out of the kitchen, and hugged her hard. She buried her head in my shoulder and breathed slowly, deeply. We stood there wrapped in each other like we'd just escaped from a horror movie, our eyes shut tight from whatever might be waiting for us.

The terror wasn't in any way gone from me. I couldn't help wondering what exactly it was acid did to your brain, and wondering how she'd been able to see the same impossible thing I saw. Were these things really there? She said she could see them all the time, but acid just opened up the possibilities for normal people, like me.

While I was thinking about all this, I became aware of another presence in the room. An invasive, cold, ominous presence. I opened my eyes. Her mother was standing in front of us sipping her wine and watching us like we were a bad stage performance, as we were deeply entangled, shaking and petting each other.

"What is this, *The Children's Hour*? What's wrong with you?" She raised her right eyebrow at her daughter. "I've been looking all over for you. I thought you were upstairs."

"I've just been having a headache, Mom."

I realized that she must be used to her daughter's bouts of . . . whatever, but she treated her daughter's apparent disarray with nothing more than a little annoyance and feigned ignorance.

"Well then, have a seltzer. You're probably dehydrated. There are some bottles in the fridge."

"*I'll* get it," I said abruptly, and skipped back into the kitchen.

I heard her mother through the door. "Pull yourself together. We've been planning a surprise for you. I mean, you don't *have* to do it, even though we've been planning it all week. I mean, if you really don't feel like it, dear."

"Planning what?" I stepped back in and handed her the seltzer. She unscrewed the lid, gulped down half the bottle, then burped.

"There, that's more like it," her mother encouraged her. "Have a seat." She walked her daughter over to the dining room table and dimmed the lights. Waving her hand in the air at no one, she hollered, "All right! She's ready!"

What ensued was the strangest and dorkiest ritual I have ever been privy to, live or on video, ever. Ten Mensans marched in slowly, in single file, singing the philosophers' drinking song from *Monty Python's Flying Circus* at the speed and tone of a druidic hymn. It was creepy. They then found their places standing around Kali, who was seated at the table. She was smiling her overwide smile and laughing a silent laugh that looked like little convulsions. When they had all made their way in, they stopped singing and declared happily, three times in unison, "One of us! One of us! One of us!" before placing the twenty-page IQ test on the table in front of her. This IQ test would decide if she could become an official member of Mensa or not, and I knew this was the single most important thing in the world to her: to be acknowledged as a fellow genius by her parents' friends. I just didn't think this was something she should undergo while peaking on acid.

Liz handed her a pen. Her mother nodded approvingly. "I don't think you should do this right now," I tried. "You're not feeling well." Her dilated eyes smiled up at the Mensans. Totally ignoring my comment, she tore open the paper that kept the sides of the booklet sealed, then beamed up at them, shaking with apparent joy and surprise. "Of course I'll do it," she said. "I am. I'm one of you."

⊙ ⊙ ⊙

I'm still circling this East St. Louis strip. I've taken to waving back at the whores. They are very polite. This is my last time around, though. I'm gonna go ahead and drive to my hometown for the night. To hell with this.

She failed the test, of course. And the rest, it's hard to explain. She just sat there quietly in the car as we drove away from the house and the scene of her worst embarrassment. When they tallied the results and announced them, her mother just quietly excused herself from the party. She started trembling, and the other guests comforted her, saying that she could try again soon, that she just wasn't feeling well. But she bombed. Of course she did. She was tripping. I drove her home in a drug haze, finally starting to come down, and she didn't say a word until we got into the apartment, and then, well, I finally got to meet Rose, the person she becomes who does things she doesn't remember doing.

The apartment is destroyed. Most of her breakable things are broken, in pieces. There is a golf-ball-sized welt on her head (her own doing, not mine) and I have a swollen jaw, and she is sleeping now, as a result of many anti-anxiety medications I insisted she take so she would stop ramming herself headfirst into the walls and tearing her things to pieces. I am driving this disgusting strip of a road, over and over again, trying to figure where to go for the rest of the night . . . for the rest of my life.

There's that fucking song playing on the radio, the one that always made me think of her, even when I was with her. I should have noticed this as a sign before tonight—*"Where all the bodies hang on the air"*—that's not a sweet song at all. The fact that this is the song I most associate with my romantic relationship, there is definitely something very wrong with that. She's gonna miss me. She destroyed everything else. She's gonna tell me she can't go on without me. And she probably can't. Pretty soon now, though, I won't really care. I crossed the waters. I'm gonna go home through the town. I'll pass the shadows that fell down from when we met. But I'm gone from there.

WHAT'S HAPPENING ON THE NEWS?

When I was in the fourth grade, our teacher's twenty-year-old son visited our class to present an educational show-and-tell. He brought in a helmet full of sand. He was a soldier. It was a Desert Storm helmet. He poured the sand out into a Ziploc bag. He said, "This sand is from Iraq." We awed. Iraq was so far away and on the news. We had our simulacra experience. We were ten and didn't know what it meant. He passed the helmet around. We laid hands on it. We all touched it with our hands like it might be healing us or transmitting some wisdom from far-off, soon-to-be-conquered places through war-armor osmosis. There was an indentation in the helmet. Our teacher's son said the indentation was from a bullet. The helmet was bulletproof. We imagined his head in the sand in Iraq as we placed small hands silently on the helmet. It was an act of worship. He was a hero and we were worshiping his headdress.

He told us a story about another head, not his own, Saddam Hussein's head. He said the army had secretly put a bounty on Saddam Hussein's head, one million dollars to any soldier who delivered. I raised my hand. I wanted to know if Saddam Hussein's head should be delivered on a platter or a stick. I was a child familiar with the Bible. In biblical stories, heads are often delivered on platters, and sometimes left as warnings on sticks. He said that "the bounty on Saddam Hussein's *head*" wasn't literal, that it just meant they wanted him dead, but if a soldier brought back Saddam Hussein's head without the body, that would have been acceptable, too. That soldier still would have received the million dollars. This information about the bounty, he told us, was a secret, because it wasn't technically legal. It would be a war crime. But it shouldn't be, because Saddam Hussein was very bad.

He opened the Ziploc bag of sand. We formed a line, and, one at a time, walked up to him and poked our fingers in the sand. Now we could say we'd touched sand from Iraq, so far away and on the news.

Tyson was in line right in front of me. Our last names began with letters at the end of the alphabet, so we did everything last, together. Tyson poked his fingers in the sand solemnly, then pulled his fingers out and stepped away. I stepped up next. I poked my finger in the sand, fingering a souvenir of war below the fourth-grade blackboard. It was minuscule and cool like the sand on any beach. But it was desert sand, Desert Storm sand. I pulled my finger out, then followed Tyson to the back of the room where we sat in our end-of-the-alphabet-last-name seats. He turned around and said, "That's a great movie idea. Someone should make a movie about a soldier cutting off Saddam Hussein's head." I nodded, but couldn't immediately think of any part I might play in this film of his. The role of "soldier's wife" would most likely only include the most minimal side scenes, and I was interested in major roles.

Tyson wanted to be a film director, but like the kind that writes his own scripts and then directs them. His family was Italian, although hundreds of years removed from Italy, so he loved *The Godfather*, and *GoodFellas*, and *Scarface*. He loved Quentin Tarantino, and Spike Lee, and Woody Allen, too. He loved any director that a kid who wanted to be a serious film director in the US was supposed to like. He had wanted to become this thing, a serious yet entertaining film director, since he was eight years old. That's all he wanted to do and mostly all he talked about, except for one girl who he was in love with since he was like five, and the fact that his family was Italian. Those were his three subjects: films, Emily Spencer, and being tenuously Italian.

We got along. I wanted to be an actress and Tyson said, when we grew up, I could definitely act in his movies. Most of the types of films he was interested in making called for a quirky and fiery redheaded female lead. I was a shoo-in. I wanted to be a Christian actress, and the first thing I wanted to know when we began discussing this collaboration was if he would be making any Christian films. There aren't really any gangster Christian films, and he said he probably wouldn't be making the breakout gangster Christian film, but that he wouldn't be making any *anti*-Christian films, either. That was good enough for me. Tyson and I had a plan.

When I was ten, I wanted to grow up to be a Christian actress and live in the little yellow house next door to my parents. That was my plan. With Tyson, I had at least one other person besides my parents invested in some portion of my plan. Dialogue-driven gangster movies were okay, as long as I didn't cuss in them. In order to be a good Christian actress, I didn't have to do *only* Christian films, just as long as I didn't do any anti-Christian films, and I was a Christian myself and spread the word of the Lord through my fame, that was enough to keep me qualified as a Christian actress.

It is hard to be a Christian actress. My mother warned me that when I got to Hollywood, I would have to contend with the gay mafia. If I didn't sometimes pretend to be gay, she warned me, I might not get any good roles . . . because of the gay mafia. But even if it meant struggling for years, I couldn't pretend to be gay, because the fate of my immortal soul rested on not doing that. When she invoked the gay mafia, I pictured men who looked and dressed like the people in the movies my friend Tyson wanted to make—large men with scarred faces wearing tailored suits, mysterious fedoras, and ostentatious gold jewelry, only being much nicer to one another than those men. That's what the gay mafia was in my head: Al Pacino giving Marlon Brando sweet little kisses on the cheek.

There were many other reasons it was going to be hard to be a Christian actress. I watched a lot of Christian talk shows with my mom, and they interviewed a Christian actress on one of these shows. The actress told the hosts everything about just how difficult it is to be a Christian actress. She couldn't get many leading roles, because she refused to do any nudity or profanity. This made it hard, she said, because so much of Hollywood was working for secular values, which often intersect with the values of Satan. She traced her path to Christianity and talked about coming of age in a family of "holiday Christians"—Christians who only went to church on Easter and Christmas. These people, her family, didn't practice their beliefs in their everyday life. She was now living a true Christian life, imbuing each choice and moment of her life with a Christian conscientiousness. That's why she wouldn't do sex scenes in movies.

She told the hosts that because she was raised by holiday Christians, no one ever talked to her about the evils of sex when she was younger, so she had sex outside of marriage when she was in her late teens. The hosts gasped and guffawed. She told them, the first time she had sex, she didn't even know what it was. "The first time I had sex," she said, "I didn't even know I was having sex. I had sex and didn't even know I'd had it. I didn't know what it was. I found out after the fact, when I told a friend about what had happened. I was like, 'Huh, that was sex?' Not only did I not know how sacred or precious an act it was, I didn't even know *what* it was."

This revelation by the Christian actress made my mom very nervous. My mother made sure I knew exactly what sex was so that I would never accidentally have it.

There are many types of sex not to have. Sex is when a man puts his penis in a woman's vagina, and that is basic. Basic sex not to have is basic sex outside of marriage. Just because you are married, though, doesn't mean you can have sex with anyone. Adultery is sex not to have with someone you are not married to if you or they are married. There is sex *never to have* under any circumstances, for which there are grave punishments. Homosexual sex is sex never to have and no one ever explained to me the exact functionality of the majority of homosexual acts, except to occasionally invoke male anuses and cringe. Worse than homosexual sex is sex with animals, and in the Bible, dirty women who committed bestiality with dogs were led in chains like dogs before the king and stoned, righteously. Worse than this was sex with oneself, or masturbation, which is the dirtiest, lowest form of sex never to have, ever, and, I have found, the easiest of all of them to have accidentally.

I spent some serious time wondering how the Christian actress could have had basic sex not to have accidentally. After she divulged this information about accidentally having sex in her late teens, the Christian television talk show hosts looked at the Christian actress like she had two heads, and with deep concern. I could tell they were thinking she wasn't smart. But I knew she was.

I knew that in order to be an actress you have to be very, very intelligent, because acting is the highest form of art. Getting the expression just right. Manifesting another's consciousness, emotional history, and mannerisms, and blending all of these factors into one perfect moment of realizing you are in love with the man you thought was an oaf, or that the world is about to end because of a meteorite that's headed directly toward the Earth; or deep surprise, wide-eyed shock at the revelation of a long-kept family secret about a faked-death inheritance. Acting is pure alchemy. It is an art that is so near a science and nothing deserves more reverence, which is why we celebrate actors above all other artists. Actors preserve and illustrate our history and are the harbingers of our future social, emotional, and intellectual evolution. Like Andie MacDowell.

Andie MacDowell is a serious artist. If only she'd used her power and fame for good. Not that she used it for evil. It was just hard for me to respect and admire her as much as I did while keeping in mind the basic fact that she did not imbue her daily actions and choices with Christian conscientiousness.

She'd never even publicly proclaimed that she was a Christian, and *Sex, Lies, and Videotape* was arguably an anti-Christian film. But *Curly Sue*, *Green Card*, and *Groundhog Day*, those films were works of high art and also worthy of moral respect. When, in *Groundhog Day*, Andie MacDowell first views the ice sculpture Bill Murray has impeccably chiseled as her face, what other portrait of Cupid's sting has been so authentic as her brown eyes jutting like two blushing twins skating upon the realization of love in the apocalyptically repeated dusk of that eternal night of romantic comedy? None so much.

It was hard for me to boycott *Sex, Lies, and Videotape*, because I loved Andie MacDowell truly, and respected her as an artist and had to forgive her, because I knew it was part of the artistic temperament to make less than scrupulous decisions, on occasion. It was not hard to boycott Madonna. She was never an artist. She was just filthy for the sake of being filthy. It was slightly difficult to boycott Kmart, which was a boycott led by the entire Southern Baptist church for nearly eight years. That boycott occurred because Kmart sold novels in which basic sex outside of marriage between teenagers was portrayed in a positive light. Some secular people also said that the boycott happened because Jerry Falwell and other members of the Southern Baptist Convention owned stock in Walmart. That, though, was a coincidence, and Walmart was a righteous store, so it would make sense that righteous men would invest in it. The first few years of the boycott of Kmart was hard, because sometimes there were things at Kmart that we couldn't get at Walmart. Soon enough, though, after the boycott spread to other Christian denominations in our area, the local Kmart shut down and Walmart grew into a Super Walmart, and they always had everything we needed in stock. So that was a boycott that was only mildly inconvenient to me.

Almost all of the boycotts were easy enough for me: *Barney*, *Dungeons & Dragons*, karate, yoga, the metric system. I boycotted all of those things and all of those boycotts were fine. Only one boycott truly shook my devotion—the boycott of Troll dolls. Troll dolls were a difficult boycott for me.

Like I said, I was very familiar with the Bible and was raised Southern Baptist, which involved a lot of boycotts. It involved a lot of protests, and a lot of paying attention to what was happening in the world, in order to try and guess how near the end times really were. My parents and I watched a lot of Christian talk shows and Christian news shows on the Christian News Network, which is not the same as the secular CNN, which is a fact I found out the hard way.

When I was seven, "CNN" reported that the Russians had dug a manhole too deep, and they had dug all the way into Hell, and a demon had risen out of the hole bearing a sign that read, in Russian, "I have risen." I was obviously very upset by this. An open hole in the world letting out the demons of Hell is very upsetting to a seven-year-old. I went to school all worked up, and in front of the whole class asked the teacher if she'd heard the news on CNN. She couldn't exactly debunk it, because it was part of my religion, but I gathered from her tone and response and the looks on the faces of the other students that I wasn't getting the same news they were. When I returned home, I learned that this demon rising out of a Russian manhole had been nothing more than a prank by some graffiti artists. They'd made a fourteen-foot-tall papier-mâché statue of a demon holding a hand-painted sign and placed it in a hole at a construction site. Blurry images of this had been mistaken by CNN for the real thing. It was still possible that the graffiti artists responsible were Russian Satanists, and we should let this be a warning that the Russians were, as always, up to no good. This misreporting did not dissuade my family in any way from our adamant devotion to Christian news and talk shows.

We liked Christian talk shows so much we even attended a live taping of *Action Sixties* in 1990 as part of our summer vacation. *Action Sixties* was a Christian talk show that was partially responsible for the boycott of Troll dolls, *Dungeons & Dragons*, and *Barney*. The episode we attended was on the theme of occult toys, and featured a teenager who had attempted to kill his parents because of a sort of *Dungeons & Dragons*–inflicted dementia that was not unlike demon possession. He had actually spent time in juvenile detention for this attempted murder of his parents, and came on the show to speak out against the evils of magical role-playing board games.

Two years after we attended the taping of this show, a friend of the family bought me the *Dungeons & Dragons* board game as a birthday present. Mom had told me to be polite no matter how I felt about any gift I received, but opening that was hard. I was terrified. This game made kids kill their parents. I didn't want to kill anybody. I thanked the people for the gift, but when everyone left, Mom and I had to decide whether it would be best to return *Dungeons & Dragons* and replace it with a more wholesome birthday present, or to burn it and so subtract one object of evil from the world.

We burned it in the trash pile behind the garage. I expected to hear the wailing of wayward spirits making their way up to the starry country night sky as the cardboard crackled. To my disappointment, I heard nothing of the sort. Just some smoke and the non-demon-possessed sound of plastic popping.

Action Sixties did quite an in-depth series on occult toys over the years. It is a little-known fact that many members of the pagan occult are toy manufacturers, and own numerous design companies and movie studios. There are real witches in the world, real pagans running the gamut from Wiccans, to Satanists, to demonologists, and they attempt to subliminally influence children through cartoons and by embedding magical objects disguised as toys in ordinary homes.

This is what happened with Troll dolls, and I have to admit, this was difficult for me, as this occurred at a time when I was beginning to waver in my constant, righteous devotion to Christ. An adamant evangelical Christian with an obsession with perfect grammar, and an unfortunate perm, was a difficult thing to be in junior high.

I was being unfortunate in multiple ways in the seventh grade when *Action Sixties* featured interviews with three kids, teens and preteens, claiming that they had been woken up in the middle of the night by demon-possessed Troll dolls. All the kids said the dolls' eyes glowed red. One boy said the dolls told him to kill his parents. Another girl said that the dolls spoke to her in an unknown language, which her mother believed to be a demonic language.

I had quite a large collection of Troll dolls, both brand-name and generic, as well as three collector's edition Cabbage Patch Kids plush Troll dolls. I loved these dolls.

The smoke from that fire, I didn't want to watch. I didn't stay to hear if I could catch the sound of wayward spirits leaking out of their beady eyes or seeping through their bejeweled belly buttons. I walked away, head hung, arms folded, mourning a pile of much-wished-upon plastic tokens of nineties kid-hood, soon to be Christian righteousness goo.

This is not how I described the incident to my friends. I guess I felt that if I had to burn all my Troll dolls, I wanted them to think it was at least of my own volition, and, furthermore, I wanted everyone else to do it too. If I couldn't have them, no one should. I told my friends they were walking on thin ice keeping those dolls around. I told them about the kids who shared testimony on *Action Sixties*, after the Troll dolls had told them to kill their parents. I told them the dolls were tools of the occult, and were possessed by wicked spirits, and that they should be burned.

Two days before seventh-grade graduation, I opened up my locker, and an avalanche of Troll dolls spilled out. Green-headed and rainbow belly-button-bejeweled plastic, pot-bellied Trolls fell around me like pop-fad raindrops, landing at my feet and bouncing along the tiled floors of the hall. Everyone pointed and stared and started laughing, shouting out mean things like, "Be careful. They're going to get you! They're possessed! She thinks Troll dolls are real!"

They hadn't understood a thing I'd said.

The fact that they were in my locker meant one of my good friends had been part of it, because they were the only ones who knew my combination. I felt completely betrayed. They were all Christians, too. But sometimes I felt like we didn't worship the same God. My God was much more serious than theirs, and at the same time, my God was a joke to them.

My God had been coming under more and more scrutiny by godless members of my now godless nation. When George

Bush was president, there was God in the White House. I cried both times Clinton was elected, sobbed like someone was dying. Someone *was* dying—thousands of unborn each year—and Clinton and Gore were baby killers, out-and-out, unapologetic. Under their rule, the persecution of Christians increased tenfold. This was no surprise. Since I could remember, I'd been told that I should expect increasing persecution as a Christian. But it was hard to take. During one of the pro-life rallies I attended during the eighth grade, several women attempted to rush our life chain. In case you don't know what a life chain is, it's when pro-life demonstrators link arms to form a human chain around an abortion clinic. These women shouted obscenities at us and flipped us their middle fingers and tried knocking us over. The police intervened, but I couldn't believe the brazenness of the women. All the years before, when I'd attended rallies at abortion clinics, the women shuffled in, heads hung, hiding their faces. The only way to commit knowing sin is with your head hung. These women, though, during the Clinton administration, they acted like they weren't even doing anything wrong. They acted like *we* were the ones who were wrong. It was real religious war. The other side was fighting for their own damnation.

My absolute favorite talk show host, Jack Van Impe, and his wife and cohost, Rexella, the founders of Ministries International, had warned that this sort of fighting would begin to occur. Jack Van Impe is a Revelations scholar who broadcasts a Christian news show out of Michigan. He knows about holy wars and the increasing persecution Christians will be facing as the Second Coming grows nigh. Christians have to fight to make way. As it is foretold in Revelations, when Israel controls the Dome of the Rock, which is currently controlled by Palestine, the Muslim nations will rise up against the reigning Christian nation, and Jesus will return. This is why it is so important that Israel take back all of the Palestinian territory. George Bush secretly hired Jack Van Impe as one of his foreign policy advisers. That made us feel very comforted, knowing someone we trusted had the president's ear. Bill Clinton only gave lip service to Israel's cause, and, as far as I could tell, did not seem concerned with events that needed to occur to bring on the Second Coming of Christ.

When I was in the eighth grade, Clinton was president. There were no wars in the eighth grade, save the ongoing unseen holy war between good and evil. There was no Desert Storm. The surface of the sand stood still. America was engaged in no war, so there were *no* wars. The road to the rapture was on pause. The hourglass frozen in midair. The sand stood still. A soldier stood before us, once again, fidgeting with a duffel bag. "Boys," he told the boys, "in about four years, you'll be old enough to be drafted." Usually if something was only available to the boys, the girls protested the unfairness of the situation. Everyone kept quiet here. "Boys and girls," he told us all, "in about four years, you'll be deciding whether to go to college or get a job. There are a lot of big choices ahead of you." He produced a gas mask. It looked like an elephant head. He asked for a volunteer. One of the boys went up and the soldier showed us how to wear and use the gas mask. He placed it over the boy's head. The boy looked like a weird elephant-headed god. He waved his arms, clowning. We giggled.

"How many of you want to go to college?" the soldier asked us. Less than half of us raised our hands. I lived in a rural farm town of a thousand people. There were two hundred kids in my school, which housed the seventh to twelfth grades, and combined the populations of three towns: mine, and the neighboring hamlets.

Most of our families didn't have money for us to go to college. Most of our parents hadn't attended college. Some of our parents hadn't even completed high school. There were a few farms to be inherited. There was the cement factory, and the car parts factory in the next town over. There were two gas stations, and one dollar store. There was also nursing and teaching. These were mostly our options. In my entire class, two people would go on from graduation directly to a four-year college. One of them (me) would drop out the first year.

"For those of you who raised your hands, and also for those of you who didn't, college is a great opportunity. You know, if you join the military, you can go to basically any college you want, and I mean for free. We pay for it. If you go to college, that means you can get whatever job you want when you're older. Think about that." We thought about that. We were thirteen- and fourteen-year-olds thinking about it.

"What do you want to do when you grow up?" he pointed to Josh. In two years, Josh would be dead. Beginning my eighth-grade year, each year, one student in my school would die, and also, one girl would get pregnant, so I guess it evened out. It was a stable population.

The deaths were all unrelated to each other. My freshman year, Justin drowned in the creek while swimming with my two boyfriends. My sophomore year, Josh got depressed and rammed his hot wheel at eighty in a twenty, twisting his car around the American flagpole in the town triangle (we didn't have a square, we had a triangle) set between warring gas stations. He was sixteen and they say his head smashed clear through the hole in the steering wheel like the wane reduction of a cat slipping between impossible openings. The girls got dressed up to cry in the tiled halls, like a gathering of distressed school birds, and we all discovered who had really loved him before they slew each other over which one had worn the most scandalous skirt to his funeral. My junior year, Blaine sucked the barrel of a shotgun after blowing the fine white globe of his two-year-old daughter's skull to bits. His ex-girlfriend, the child's mother, threatened the school populace with unnamed punishment if they attended his funeral. Her daughter's coffin was so small, and the mother only eighteen. I remember her in study hall looking like a thin succession of lines meeting at a shivering torso, bent mourning a dead child over SAT books.

My senior year, my brother's best friend died because of a broken arm. His arm got an infection under the cast where it had been stitched. His mother had spent so much money on the initial emergency room visit, she didn't want to go back to the hospital, thinking his arm would heal on its own. He died from a gangrene infection. Two years after I graduated, the valedictorian of the class below me overdosed on heroin and meth in her living room with her one-year-old daughter in her arms.

But this was not yet. None of this had happened yet, and live Josh, handsome still-living Josh, sat with his mop of blond hair and hopeful fourteen-year-old eyes sparkling, as the soldier pointed, commanding him to contemplate what he wanted to be when he grew up. He wanted to be a veterinarian or an engineer. He wasn't sure. The soldier told him he could learn engineering in the military. He pointed to Tyson and asked the same question. Tyson puffed up his chest. "I'm going to be a film director and write my own scripts," he proudly announced.

There is a moment, for every child, when the adults around them, either one by one or collectively, decide that the child's dreams must be obliterated. Adults do this so that they can replace the noble and ridiculous aspirations of children with the ignoble and ridiculous aspirations of grown-ups. They do this because they too, in a moment where they were on the other end of this awful thing they are doing, were taught that only the most ignoble and ugly things are attainable. For this reason, disappointment with one's life becomes a much more believable outcome. And, as Americans hate failure, this actually becomes the grudging goal of how one's life should be lived—passing the time with hated tasks, thankful and even possessive of the most basic aspects of survival: family, roof, clothing, food.

The soldier turned his jealous eyes on Tyson's dream. "You need to go to college to learn to direct and write scripts. How do you plan to pay for that?"

"His family owns the grocery store *and* the bar," Emily, Tyson's lifelong love, chirped from the front of the room, shooting Tyson an approving smile.

"That's great," the soldier nodded, "but have you thought about this realistically?" Tyson shifted in his chair. "Do you know how many people want to go to Hollywood and direct films?"

"I guess a lot," Tyson croaked out. The wrecking ball was swinging toward him. He wasn't ducking in time.

"Millions," the soldier answered, as if accusing Tyson of something. "And do you know how many people actually get to go off and direct films in Hollywood?"

"Not a lot," Tyson said, dejected.

The soldier pursed his lips as if in apology, "About point zero, zero, one percent of the people who want to do that." And then he added, "Every little girl wants to be a ballerina. But there's only one part for the swan."

The class giggled. Tyson looked like he'd been punched in the gut. I prayed that the soldier wouldn't ask me any questions. The soldier turned to the blackboard and chalked the words, all in caps: BE *ALL* YOU CAN BE. "What do you think about that?" he asked the entire class.

The first time I ever saw the line in the sky that the airplanes make, trailing steam behind them, I didn't know what it was. I saw the trail, but not the plane. The plane was long gone, but the trail was there. I didn't know what it was, but I thought I did. I was eight years old. I was raised preparing for the apocalypse. I saw that long, thin white line in the sky, and I thought the sky was splitting open. I thought it was the tear in the sky that Jesus ripped and was about to come flying through, occurring right over my house. I ran inside screaming, "The sky is opening! Jesus is coming down! Come look!" My family shouted, "Dear God!" and "Praise the Lord!" They waved hands above their heads and held their hearts. Four of my adult family members ran out on the lawn with me. We all looked up for Jesus flying down on a horse through the torn sky. "Where?" Mom shouted. I pointed to the line. The air was let out of everyone. They shook their heads. The blush began to leave their cheeks. They told me what that line was. It was not the Apocalypse coming of Christ. No rapture for the saved, no tribulation, just steam from an airplane. An airplane was not the end of the world as we knew it.

When the first plane hit the first tower, I was eighteen and becoming a nonbeliever. When the first plane hit the first tower, I was asleep in my room, dreaming that I was a black, male vampire in a coffin and someone was slowly running a wooden stake through my heart. When the second plane hit the second tower, my dad woke me up, screaming about what was happening. *September 11* was happening. I went to the television. I watched the smoke billowing out and the little specks of bodies leaping and falling from the buildings with the sky-blue sky doing nothing to help behind them. The part of me that still unwillingly believed expected them to all halt in mid-fall and begin ascending up into the blue, into His arms. It was the rapture in reverse. Everything was falling.

Just months before high school graduation, Tyson signed up for the army, along with one other boy in our class, and two from the class below. The average class size in my school was about twenty kids per grade. Each year, at least two kids joined the military. That means at least ten percent of the students every year left high school from my town to join the military. They signed up at lunchtime. Twice a week, every year, during the last few months of school, the military set up an information and recruitment booth in the lunchroom. One after another, year after year, the boys would turn eighteen and start eyeing that booth over their ham and cheese sandwiches like it was a girl they were afraid to get fucked by. Then finally, one day, one of them would have too much Coca-Cola and he'd swagger over to the corner of the lunchroom and sign up for a private appointment at the recruiting station in the next town over. The next morning, he'd come in and announce proudly, puffing his chest, "I'm in the army, now. I'm getting outa *here*, fuckers." I think that's what they thought, that they were getting out of this Podunk town. Going to see something beautiful. Going to see the real world. Even if they were just there to bomb the real world, at least they'd get to see it first;

something that wasn't cornfields and Walmart, and bent-over grandparents heading to factories, and teen moms trying harder than anyone could bear to look at long, and church potlucks, drunken bonfires, and strip-mall parking lots and all that.

They wanted to see something spectacular. Everyone wants to live a spectacular life, live something anyone would ever make a film about. Who wants to make a film about bent-over grandparents still struggling to pay electric bills after sixty years of working, just struggling to pay bills? They probably thought bombing the real world, like the one they saw in movies, would save them from that fate too. They didn't have access to the kind of story lives where people walk around great cities falling in love at museums, or become rich spy-thieves and go on high-speed car chases, only to discover the meaning of life was hidden in a jewel behind a secret door right where they started, or the kind of story lives where people get rich starting an exciting but quirky business, or make academic dialogue over complex personal entanglements. Hell, they didn't even have access to living a college road trip film. But they did have access to Marlon Brando. They had access to ". . . it's safe to surf this beach!" and the tanks rolling over a moral dilemma, where either way, whatever they decide, they are the hero, shooting or not shooting the shivering man, the slant-eyed man, shooting up the family cowering behind torn couches and searching for the armed men hiding in the closet, trudging through the desert, *Hurt Locker, Jarhead,* pounding your girlfriend against the wall, legs spread, on leave, for God, for country, for fuck's sake, what's the other option? Either way, pull the trigger or not, they are the hero, because they just had to do it or just couldn't bring themselves to. Everyone feels compassion. There's so much weighing on their dumb, brave heads.

I remember the day Tyson made the decision. We were sitting on the bleachers in the gymnasium. The gym was empty. They'd begun hanging the decorations for graduation. There were sequined trestles lining the basketball hoop. We were eighteen and this was the most adult conversation we would ever have. He told me he was going to sign up. I asked about his life's dream, the one he was just ditching. He told me that's all it had been, a childish dream. He told me he had no experience with film. "You," he told me, "you could really be an actor. You've been acting in the community theater since you were five. You have real experience to put on your resume." This of course was ridiculous. My starring roles had been, namely, Gossip Lady Number Two in *The Sound of Music*, and a very lesbianic Peter Pan in a children's musical version of *Peter Pan*. My rural community theater experience couldn't make for an acting resume that would give me any credit in a real city, even accounting for the elite Hollywood gay mafia.

"Maybe that's *your* path. With everything that's happened in this country, I've got to step up and take responsibility. I have to defend your freedom to follow your dreams. Maybe that's my path, to make the world safe for people to grow up and do the things I always wanted to do."

When people begin to talk in words you've heard before, it's easy to know who's writing the script. I'd seen words like those on pamphlets, and heard the meaning of them in my own speech as a child. I'd heard these words on the real news, the Christian news, and from the mouths of young military recruiters who stood in the corner of the lunchroom below helicopter explosion posters trying not to look like they were checking out high school girls. And now it was coming from Tyson, the aspiring, serious yet entertaining Italian film director. And I realized what I always should have known when I looked at the certainty and question battling in Tyson's wide, baby blue eyes, and his dimples showing even when there was no glimmer of a smile on his face, his boyish face with the impossibly clear, smooth skin, and his wavy black hair ending in curlicues on his forehead. He wasn't a director at all. He was the leading man. He was the one everyone was rooting for. And it *was* a gangster Christian film he was starring in, after all. The movie opened up before me. I could see all the scenes:

Tyson in Iraq pressing buttons, and buildings miraculously exploding hundreds of miles away. Tyson standing in uniform in Baghdad, machine-gun-armed, passing day after day, just watching out. Tyson running in combat boots, the sand scattering in clouds behind him.

He wrote home, sending a letter addressed to all of his friends that Emily transcribed and emailed. He told us how he guarded a building in Baghdad when the military had taken over. He made friends with the local kids. He taught them about America. He talked to the Iraqi children about Jesus, and about owning cars and houses, and playing video games. He taught them how to say the word "tits." He taught them what it meant. They thought it was awful, then they thought it was hilarious.

This movie he starred in, it had side characters as well. Their stories would not end in triumph like the one of the leading man. A year into service, another boy from our town who served with Tyson was sent home on permanent leave for mental instability. He got a job delivering pizza in the next town over. He was fired after six months for repeatedly telling customers gory details about the war, how his job in Iraq was to shoot his friends in the ankles during house raids. This was his job, because he never "froze" during raids. (He would always be proud of that.) Many of his fellow soldiers just froze during crossfire, stood staring dumbly into the oncoming blaze. So his job was to notice when this happened and then shoot his friends in the ankles so they would fall down and not get shot in the head and killed during crossfire when they froze, which he never did, which he was always very proud of.

A boy from the class above me, who became a military medic, was dishonorably discharged for servicing a severely wounded Iraqi civilian before servicing a mildly wounded US soldier during one of these raids. He would come home to the town he had grown up in and live in the house he purchased before leaving for Iraq. Within a month, his wife would leave him for another man, the one she started seeing while he was in Iraq. He would start getting drunk at local bars and telling people the story of his dishonorable discharge, over and over. Five years after losing his home to foreclosure, he swallowed a handful of pills, and was simply gone.

Tyson got shot in the leg and returned with a Purple Heart. The leading man in his American gangster Christian film, he returned a war hero. The town put a sign up for him in front of the high school, welcoming him home, naming him a hero. He was famous in the town. He got loans. He bought a nice house and married Emily. He took over ownership of his family's grocery store. He had three children. They were baptized in the Catholic church. He bought a Jet Ski. He stayed fit, except for a beer belly that formed in his mid-thirties. In his mid-thirties, the war was still going, going in a crusade against an ever-expanding enemy. Victory had been declared numerous times. And he thought it was a victory, in a way, for himself at least. His house was two stories tall, with a swimming pool, and game room, and shiny new cars always in the driveway. He was a local hero. He rode at the head of the military float in the town's bicentennial parade. He stood next to the mayor when the ribbon was cut in front of the new library. And once a year, he visited the fourth-grade class in the school he'd attended as a child. He brought in his Purple Heart. He brought in the bullet shell that had been embedded in his leg. The class passed it around from one to another and awed. It was a miraculous token of war heroism, manifested before them from overseas, from a place that seemed so far away, and sometimes even, on the news.

A LITTLE ASIDE

The sky is blood. I know you probably don't see it that way. Most people probably don't see it that way. But I see it clear for what it is. That's how I see things; clear for what they are, and that's how I know what the sky is, 'cause I ain't afraid to look at it and see it for what it is. Things have a way of showing you their true selves when they're transitioning. Their true selves is there in the moment between, when they go into the space between, like how the moment between calm and anger, you see what a person really is; if they are a scared person, or a sad person, or just a hard motherfucker. In that moment between things it's all, we're all just changing clothes, putting on a new cloak, a new mask to play out the next part. And if you look close, and if you train yourself to look most close at those moments, you get to see the bare body under it all while it's changing. You see what it really is underneath that's wearing that mask. I only look at the sky during the time between day and night, when the sun's going down and it's spilling red, that's the bare body of it, the truth of it all, pink and red and spreading open. The sky is blood. We're just wading around under a big pulsing ball of blood. I know that. I looked at it clear. The sky is blood. But the hell of it is, it's our blood up there.

I know other things about the world I seen from looking at it clearly too, ain't many others seen. For instance, I know the sea is the night. I known that blackbirds are bruises given by loved ones. Grass is fire. Snakes are your innocence daring you to kill it. Paintings are tombstones, and tombstones don't even exist, except for trees, which are the real tombstones. Stars are old men. The only thing I found that is what it is is guilt. Guilt is guilt. Romantic love is never love, but it can be just about anything else. Children are funhouse mirrors that ain't no fun really. Mountains are turmoil. Cornfields are the vulgarity of lust spread thin and hiding. Peace is everywhere that we aren't. Fish are God in little pieces. God is a bunch of little fish looking like a big whale. Teeth are the same as toenails. Sex is rest. Pain is pi. Strength is falling. And freedom is not being in fucking jail.

They put me in here this afternoon. I still ain't got to talk to a fucking lawyer even though they told me they appointed me one. I ain't seen no lawyer. Where the hell is he? I'd like to know. I've been in here for three goddamned days. They told me I have the right to speak to an attorney. Well, how's about it? I'm ready. I got time! God knows I got time. Those state-appointed lawyers don't give a shit about you anyway. I think half the time they *want* me to go to jail just as much as the prosecutors, really. Damn.

Sometimes I feel like a big red bird on fire, like an American flag on fire, like a big red bird tearing out from the red stripes of the flag on fire.

The feeling of guilt is one thing, but the state of being guilty is a whole 'nother. I feel guilty about a lot of things, but I ain't guilty of nothing. What do they got on me? An empty baggie that could've been full of anything. Bath salts? What do they know? They don't know nothing. Said I was acting weird in the Walmart parking lot. Well, is that a crime? Is acting weird a crime? Last time I checked, that weren't fucking illegal. They want me to say some shit, I know, want me to say some shit so they can put me away for god knows what. Probably want me to say something that they can call me a terrorist for. The FBI got my number. They call me and pretend to have the wrong number, asking for people with made-up names: Angelina Georgina, Tammy Hall, Candy Hill. Those sound like real names to you? Fuck no. They just want to hear my voice. Catch me saying something I shouldn't. They're recording everything. People laughed at me for years when I told them, but it came out, it's true. I was right about it all and they ain't laughing no more. I don't know why more people don't care about that.

They been testing bombs on the moon, and no one cares, though we didn't get a chance to vote on it. Democracy, my ass. I know about it. They're mining up there; Obama and Putin and the pope, they're mining up there, even though they told *us* the moon don't have no resources. I know what things are. I read about it.

The world is full of evil men. Evil people are blending in with the good ones, pretending to be good. I read some people think there are lizard aliens taking human form and running our government. But they ain't just in the government. They're everywhere. When I was little, I saw them. They showed me what they were. My dad's friends when I was little, took me out, hunting they said, and took me instead into an old shack in the woods and showed me what they were. Shape-shifting demons, and the blood sky and the blood dirt; it ain't what they're from.

I know what things are. I look at them the moment between, when they're thinking, finishing or starting and I see what they are. They got jagged teeth and they look like a horned scaly creature. That's what Dahmer's victims said he did. Shifted shape. They're around.

There are lots of things. I know when it's coming. I know when it's gonna happen: 12/21/2121. We don't got much time left. You ever hear that old song that was written about what Nostradamus predicted? It goes, *"Blackbird singing in the dead of night."*

I just want my family with me when it happens. What if it's really in 2021? If it happens sooner, when we're still alive, we'll just tuck our heads in tight and think about the wormhole so we go with the light, together. I'll pray to Jesus to take us through that wormhole, into the light.

I've seen the rainbows on things dancing and singing. It's a sign from God, like He sent before the Great Flood, but tiny ones, instead of one big one. I got my shit ready to go. They better let me out of here. They ain't got nothing to hold me on.

Free country, my ass. My fucking ass it is.

A NEW MOHAWK

M ost of the Mohawks in America are unincorporated territories, areas that lie outside of any municipality or township. I didn't even know these places still existed. Apparently, unincorporated territories are either so small, destitute, or isolated that no city, town, or respectably incorporated area has found reason to claim them; neither have the people who live in these unincorporated territories seen fit to claim themselves. There's Lake Mohawk New Jersey, Mohawk Indiana, Mohawk Oregon, and Mohawk Tennessee. (These are all described as unincorporated areas.) I still can't figure quite why these places would all be named *Mohawk*, but maybe it has something to do with a Mohawk being an inherently in-between space. This last year, I've been trying to find out as much as possible about Mohawks. I looked up a lot of information. The term "Mohawk," of course, comes from a Native American tribe. The Mohawk Indians originally lived in what is now New York State. The indigenous word for their tribe meant "people of flint." "Mohawk" meant "eater of flesh." And they only wore their hair in what we now refer to as "the Mohawk" when they were preparing to go to war.

There are all kinds of Mohawk haircuts today that have nothing to do with unincorporated territories or war. You've got the bi-hawks, tri-hawks, cross-hawks, curly-hawks, faux-hawks, no-hawks, shark-fins, and my favorite, the psychobilly Mohawk, which is really just a spiky quiff, a lock of hair running down the center of the head and combed to one side. Quiff also means promiscuous woman, and I liked the idea of wearing that on my head all the time.

Maybe it was that kind of thinking that started this mess. I never did get a quiff. I don't have any of those others I named either. I'm the only person with this particular type of Mohawk I've ever met or heard of, and if more people had the kind of hair I have, I promise you, the world would be a very different place.

It was almost a year ago today. I had a huge crush on this girl, Kimberly. I'd been trailing her for a couple of weeks since we made out at this anti-Valentine's Day party. But she's a kind of wholesome do-gooding sort and was making me work for my dinner, so instead of ever inviting me out alone, she invited me to group events. On Sunday morning we cooked breakfast with Food Not Bombs and served homeless people in the park. On Friday I rode in a Critical Mass with her. It was nice going out with her those two weeks and seeing lots of people. I'd been spending too much time at my retail jobs, or alone sketching and submitting portfolios to galleries, most of which were turning me down. But to be honest, I was kinda just chasing her tail and getting nothing but community activities in return.

The third time we went out, she invited me to a political rally. She said we could go to a rock show after, so I thought, why not? I'd done my share of rallying. I cared about things. And this rally came with the added plus of a pretty girl.

The rally was about Palestine and Israel. It was back when Israel was going hog wild and just bombing the fuck out of Palestine, in retaliation for rockets being launched into Israel. I'd seen it all over the news for two days, and yeah, it was awful what was happening. But there are awful things happening everywhere all the time. Just not usually here.

So, I met Kim at the rally in Union Square. We stayed for two hours. It was nothing out of the ordinary. People were really upset and solemn and sincere. Then there were a few fiery speeches, as well as a small group of Zionists pinned in holding counter-protest signs across the street. A band played, and Kim held my hand and skipped around in a circle. One of her sandals came off and she scratched her foot, so we went to sit in the grass. I bought us two soy dogs. We ate them. Hers had relish and mustard, mine had ketchup. I'm recalling all of these banal details, because it seems so outlandish to me now just how ordinary everything was then. Nothing remotely strange happened. I keep playing that whole day and night over in my mind, trying to remember some sign of something, anything exceptional. But there was really nothing. It was an uneventful political rally that I went to because I had a crush on the girl who invited me and nothing exciting happened.

After finding a Band-Aid for Kim's foot and sitting around a little while, we went and got two cups of coffee, then headed over to this place called Arlene's Grocery for the concert. Kim did a lot of dancing. I mostly sat on the couch drinking and listening, thinking how much I missed CBGB. But then I thought maybe it wasn't CBGB I missed, but being twenty and feeling like I was really doing something drinking with a fake ID and being able to drink as much as possible without really feeling it, and most importantly, everything, absolutely everything being new and exciting.

It just doesn't feel the same listening to live rock when you're going to be thirty in a year, and your second drink is already making you more tired than drunk and you can't help but worry you're going to feel a little sick and depressed the next day. My mind started wandering to sort of existential crisis thoughts, like the fact that I'd been trying to convince art galleries that my charcoal comic strip sketches were gallery-worthy since I moved to the city, and I wasn't getting much further with that than I was nine years ago, and I can't blame it all on being a bo*i* instead of a bo*y*, and wondering if I even still really liked live rock; wondering if I even still liked anything really, 'cause the things that used to seem so exciting now seemed so commonplace. Was it actually those things I liked, or was it just the newness?

(I don't worry about that kind of stuff anymore.)

Kim came and interrupted my quarter-life drunk-think. She handed me a beer and smiled, then sat down next to me, her leg crossed in my direction, touching my knee. I remember this very clearly. She took a sip of her beer, tousled my hair and giggled. "You've got such a thick head of hair, Sheldon. It's really . . ." She paused long like she was wondering whether to say it. She's a few years younger than me and seemed to be getting pleasantly drunk. "Sexy," she said, and smiled, leaning in.

I gave her a sort of signature nod I have, and tried my best to look as sexy as she said I was through my increasingly tired version of buzzed. "Yeah," I said. "You know what I'm gonna do tomorrow? I think I'm gonna do a Mohawk again."

"No way! That could be really good." She started twisting my hair around one of her fingers. I don't think it really was at the time, but I remember it now as a mystical few moments when she kept touching my hair and talking about it, smiling too big and leaning in, giggling over nothing. The light was dim and the place smelled sweaty. The music was loud. Mediocre and insanely attractive people were dancing and beginning to make out around us. "What kind of Mohawk exactly are you going to do?" She took my brown hair in her fingers like a comb and held it up in the center, then tilted her head, trying to picture it.

"I was thinking about doing a quiff."

"A quaff?"

"No. Quiff. With an *i*."

"Quiff?"

"Yeah." I described a quiff to her and then told her that quiff also means promiscuous woman, and I said that I like having promiscuous women on my head. She blushed and went, "Mmmmmmm." Then she crawled on top of me, straddling my lap, and we made out till the band stopped playing.

We walked together to the subway. I asked her to come home with me. I really thought she would, but she said it was already two o'clock and she had things to do the next day, "Sorry." She kissed me on the cheek and went to her side of the subway. That moment really sucked. So I waited thirty minutes for the train, alone, feeling not drunk enough and too tired, frustrated and lonely, my hands shoved in my pockets, watching some junkie not fall repeatedly until the F train came. I got into my apartment and just crashed on top of the covers, in my clothes.

I usually would have slept until at least noon. But I woke up really early, like at eight o'clock. I couldn't figure out was wrong for a second, then I realized my head was itching like crazy. I sat up in bed and started manically scratching it, but that only seemed to make it worse. As I was scratching it, I was shocked to feel tons of little things moving around on my head. *Bedbugs!* I immediately thought. *Huge ones.* I stood up and pulled back the covers. They were all clean. No sign of the red plague. But god, that itching was awful. I ran to the bathroom and looked in the mirror.

I think it was Dr. Phil who said there are only about five principal events in every person's life after which they will never be the same; five events that change you forever. Like, you become a markedly different person after these things happen, and there's no going back to who you were before. I only have two, and I doubt I'll ever have any more. The first one was when I was twenty-four and I decided to do the tea and the top surgery (get my tits hacked off) and become a real boi. My second "principal event" occurred when I looked in the mirror that morning.

For a while I just stared at it. Then I started feeling around very gently patting at it with my hands, mumbling to myself, my mouth opening and closing slowly like a dying fish. I watched very closely, mesmerized by what I was seeing: the soldiers standing guard at the checkpoint, the line of cars and people at the base near my neck and the empty deserted area near the front, where, on one side, every few minutes, I thought I could make out some people shifting in the nearby bushes. I fingered the wall that ran like a Mohawk down the center of my head. It was solid, hard stone and did not give under the weight of my touching. Suddenly, I felt something singe my fingertip. I pulled my hand away and jumped back to the tiny sound of three little bombs exploding quickly. I put my hands in the air and pressed my back against the wall. I could make out the microscopic sound of screaming. Something fell from my head to the floor. I got down on my knees and pressed my cheek to the tile to get a good look. It was a little bigger than an ant. Well, I shouldn't say *it*. He was a little bigger than an ant, a miniature man wriggling on the floor, blood gurgling out of his mouth in bubbles. By the count of five, he was dead.

I jumped out of the bathroom, grabbed my keys off the table, and bolted down the stairs and onto the sidewalk, faster than I'd ever run. I didn't even think to try to get on the subway or grab a bus or even a cab. My body just started going and didn't seem to want to stop till I got where I needed to be. It only took me twenty minutes to get to my doctor's office. I'd never wanted to see a doctor so badly in my life. It seems silly to me now, that being my first inclination. But in those twenty minutes, I just kept telling myself that all I needed was a doctor.

I slammed open the glass doors and slid along the tile floor, my sneakers squeaking as I landed at the counter, panting beside the line of people waiting to fill out their forms. The man at the front desk started. "Excuse me! Can I help you?" His face went sprintingly from annoyed, to startled, to curious, to horrified as he looked me over.

"I need to do an emergency walk-in! Okay?"

He began breathing through his mouth and nodding unconsciously, the way people do when they are mesmerized by something inexplicable. The people in the line next to me were staring too. A couple of them had stepped away from me. "Uh-huh, sure. Have you . . ." his eyes scanned my head, "been here before?"

"Yeah. Yes," I hollered, leaning over the counter and pointing at his computer. "My doctor's name is Murphy. Is she in today?"

He looked from me to his computer to me again, his eyes wide. "I think so." He typed something on the screen. "Your name?"

"Sheldon. Sheldon Peters."

"Okay, your preferred pronoun?"

"What?"

"Ummm, *Mr.* Peters, is it?"

"Yes!" I shouted.

"What seems to be . . ." he paused again, just staring at me. I looked around quickly. One of the women in the line had backed all the way up to the door and was holding it open, watching me warily. "I'm sorry." He blinked and tried to smile. "What seems to be the nature of your emergency?"

"I . . . I . . ." I coughed and leaned over toward him. I pointed at my head, and I meant to whisper it, but instead I screamed, "I've got the Gaza Strip on my head!"

He shot straight up, tipping his chair over behind him, then stiffened. "We're going to get you a wheelchair," he told me brusquely. "Nurse!" He looked at me for a couple more seconds, then turned and disappeared through the door behind him, shouting for a nurse.

They were very sensitive to differences in this place. It's a special sort of clinic geared toward queer and trans people. I'm sure all the staff had been through all types of sensitivity trainings. But I could tell I was pushing their limits. The walls were calmingly purple. I tried to block out the sounds of machine gun fire and shouting, which luckily are only loud enough to hear if you get very close to me. While I was waiting for my wheelchair I read the mural on the wall. It was a quote by Audre Lorde. It read:

> Every woman has a militant responsibility to involve herself with her own health. We owe ourselves the protection of all the information we can acquire. And we owe ourselves this information before we may have a reason to use it.

I read it twice. Even though I was no longer a woman, it comforted me.

The guy came out running with a nurse and a wheelchair. The nurse shoved me down into the chair. The line parted for me and the nurse kept patting my shoulder, telling me everything was going to be okay. All the way up in the elevator, she tried to pat away my terror and hers.

The nurse who was patting me left as soon as another nurse came into the examination room. This woman was large, Rubenesque and tough looking with lots of eye makeup and a rose tattoo on her arm. "What do we have here?" She put her hand on her hip and tapped her foot. "They tell me you're a real special case. But I seen everything. I'm from the Bronx, you know. So go ahead and try me. Let's hear it."

I shrugged and directed her gaze to the top of my head. "I think I've got the Gaza Strip on my head."

She clicked her tongue, unimpressed. "*Mmmmm-hmmmm.* And what are your symptoms?" She tapped the pen on the clipboard, appearing slightly bored.

"Symptoms?"

"Mmmm-hmmm. That's what I said."

"Well, uh. It's the Gaza Strip. And it's on my head. See."

"Fine. Let me take a look." She laid the clipboard down and took me by the chin, turning my head side to side slowly, getting a good look at it, then released me.

"I don't know," she said, "that looks to me like it *might* be the Great Wall of China."

"I don't think so."

She rolled her eyes, annoyed. "Are *you* a doctor?"

"No."

"Well see now, neither am I, and that's why I *got to get* your *symptoms*. We'll let the doctor do the diagnosing, *ohhhhkay?*"

"Okay." I nodded and scratched.

"Don't you start scratching." She smacked my hand away. "That's the worst thing you could do. Now, what symptoms are you having that makes you think this is that Gaza thing?"

"Well," I thought hard. It seemed strange to think of them as symptoms. "There's a checkpoint. I mean, it seems to be a checkpoint."

"Okay." She wrote it on the paper. "Checkpoints. Go on."

"And there have been ongoing bombings mostly landing on the right side of my head."

"Bombings coming from the east going to the west?"

"I mean, that's assuming my face is south, and also depends on what area of the wall I'm dealing with here, right?"

She raised a painted brow. "Hey, we don't even know that it *is* a wall yet. Any other symptoms?"

"Yeah, well, earlier a miniature man fell out of my head, and . . . well, he seemed to have been shot, and he died."

"Dead men falling." She wrote it down and placed her pencil behind her ear. "The doctor will be here in a minute. You just hang tight."

She left the door slightly open. I could hear the news on the television in the waiting room. I walked to the door and listened. They were talking about Israel just like they had been constantly, all week. I heard the word "escalation," and then "fourth day of fighting." The doctor knocked on the wall. I went back to the wheelchair as she entered, my hands folded tensely in my lap. She smiled too big at me. I tried to force one in return.

"Hello, Sheldon, haven't seen you for a while. I hear we're having a bit of a special problem today."

It wasn't long before I realized there was nothing any doctor could do for me. First, Dr. Murphy had asked me where I got my hair done. I had to explain to her that I didn't do it on purpose. This whole thing just sprang up overnight. She kept me in there for five hours, bringing in almost all of the doctors in the building. They took my blood and urine and my entire life history. Dr. Murphy, at first, was worried it was a side effect of the tea and surgery. But they quickly ruled that out. A few of them thought it was a virus and one of them was dead set on it being a genetic mutation. But no one could come up with any definite answers. I was in and out of specialist offices for weeks. One of them even paid to have me flown to LA so he could observe me. I lived in a little room with a double-mirrored wall. He wanted to keep samples of the dead people that were falling out of my head, but I wouldn't let him. It's my body. Well? It is . . . I mean, they, are coming from my body. I let him test a few then give them back to me. It's weird, the relationship I have with them, the bodies.

At first, I was keeping them in a glass jar in my room, with the intention of throwing the jar away when it got full. But that didn't seem right. There are tough-looking guys with guns, but there are also old ladies, little kids, old men, and frail-looking people. I went to the 99-cent store by my house and I found these little glass kind of jewelry boxes. They look like pill holders, but they have like twenty-four square compartments and each compartment has a tiny little plastic sparkling jewel in it. It's just 99 cents each for one of these boxes. I guess the things are like little sequins girls collect to decorate clothes and phones and things. I bought a ton of them. When dead bodies fall, I take out a little plastic jewel and put in a dead body. I hope they don't mind sometimes when I put the Palestinians and Israelis in the same box. They have different compartments, so I think it's probably going to be all right. It doesn't happen often and who's going to know, anyway? I keep the plastic jewels in a scrapbook with a date written by each one. It's easy to do because the jewels are sticky on one side. Then, when all twenty-four little compartments are full, I find somewhere to bury the glass box. That's not easy to do. I know this all sounds morbid, but I've gotten used to having a bit of morbidity as part of my everyday life. I'm not going to say I understand what's happening there better than anyone, 'cause I don't at all, but I think I get it better than any American who's never been there.

All the specialists confirmed that the thing on my head is indeed a section of the barrier wall running along the Israel-Palestine border. The best explanation I found was from the guy in California. He deduced that these weren't the actual people from Israel and Palestine on my head, but flesh-and-blood animated replicas. It's a living-scale model. He deduced this, seeing that nothing I do, like shampooing or combing, seems to affect or hinder their actions. They are not aware of me or my head. I don't understand at all how this happened, but the specialist said something, which I wrote down, about chaos theory, and explained to me that everything only has the slightest probability of existence. He said that we know this is true because, and I wrote this down, "it is impossible to simultaneously measure the velocity and position of the divided nuclei in motion." So, he deduced, if everything only has a slight possibility of existence, then things that cannot exist have an almost equal possibility of existing. In other words, if everything is barely possible, then the impossible is not far from possible.

I feel like I've lived ten lives this last year. I've had so many opportunities to go places I never would have and speak in forums I never even imagined I'd be granted access to. After I got back from California, I had to start to try to live my life again. But it was hard. Israel and Palestine have a seven-hour time difference from New York, so it is much easier to sleep during their night than mine, because that's when my head is the quietest. Although it hardly ever seems totally quiet, I've also learned to deal with the symptoms pretty well.

Sometimes there are moments I almost forget it is there, or that it wasn't there to begin with. It sounds mostly like white noise to me now. A lot of people think I should go there, to Gaza. But that would really freak me out, being in the place, standing on the place that's standing on me.

When I got back from California, I had a ton of messages from friends and everyone. I hadn't spoken to anyone for nearly three weeks. I hadn't wanted anyone to know. I thought I could get it cured and come back like nothing had happened. But like I said, I had to go on with my life. We all do.

Kim had actually left me three messages, the first one was sweet, and the last two sounded increasingly concerned about my sudden disappearance. I was terrified of calling her, but I figured maybe she could help since she seemed to be up on the situation in the Middle East.

When she first saw it, she just sat me down on the chair and circled me, watching my head for like an hour, like it was a documentary or something. She even told me to be quiet a couple of times, bending close and trying to listen. But it's not possible to pick up any one distinct conversation. There are so many of them, and I'm sure most of them aren't speaking English. Groups of people chanting, shouting, or screaming are pretty audible to me or if you put your ear close, as are loud machines, gunshots, bombs, and things like that.

"This is amazing. This is a blessing in disguise," Kim told me, clasping her hands, looking excited and solemn. I told her I just wanted it gone. She said that she would help me. That there would have to be someone out there who could do something for me, and we could put ads up on Craigslist in lots of countries and cities. She also begged me to go speak at a rally the next day. I told her I didn't really know much about the situation in Gaza. "What do you mean?" she squealed. "It's on your head. Just speak about that. Speak from personal experience. That's the most powerful thing anyone can do."

I don't know if she's right about that, but I agreed. She offered to stay that night, finally. I told her no, though. I definitely didn't feel like doing anything with her, and I doubted it would be comfortable to sleep next to me. I hadn't told her about the falling people yet.

She was getting her bag and about to leave when it happened.

She later said she could see little rays of light like glitter bursting above the wall, and there was a sound like tiny firecrackers, then twelve people fell off of my head, onto the kitchen floor. Some of them were already dead when they landed, but a few of them were having seizures. We could see them moving for a moment before they became still.

"Oh no." Kim dropped her bag and fell to her knees, carefully inching toward them. I hung my head, ashamed. "Oh god, no," she whispered. "How is this possible?"

I shrugged, feeling like I wanted to cry, but not in front of her. She looked up at me, her eyes reddening and filling with tears. "Turn on the news." I walked over to the television and powered it on. Kim stood up and started flipping channels until she found a news station. They were talking about the economy. But it was a split screen, and on the bottom it showed live footage from Gaza. The footage was just dark and then there was a sudden burst like fireworks on the screen. "Oh my god! That's what just happened on your head!" The strip running below the footage said something about cluster bombs. "Those bastards!" Kim said. "You know what cluster bombs are?" I shook my head no. "They just disperse a bunch of tiny little *bomblets* over a wide area. It's completely indiscriminate." She wasn't really talking to me, but sort of making an outraged speech, like she was at a rally. "There's no way to use one without risking killing everyone around. They are the worst for civilian casualties. How can they say they're targeting Hamas when they're using cluster bombs, for fuck sake? The United Nations should outlaw them! I can't believe they haven't been sanctioned!" She stared down at the floor. "Oh hell, I can't believe it. You have evidence right here. We can just look and see if they're civilians."

"How can you tell?"

"If they have weapons or not." She pulled me down to the floor to inspect the tiny dead bodies, but once she got down where she could really see them, her face paled. She was completely silent just gazing at them. So was I. After a long time watching them not move, she asked me in a whisper, "What do you do with them?"

I stood up and turned off the television. "That's personal. I'm sorry, but I just want to be alone now. I'll see you in the morning at the rally."

Kim stood up and gave me a long hug. She left without saying anything else.

That first rally I did, I just got on the microphone and spoke for five minutes from my personal experience. I said how awful what was happening was, and that the fighting had to end. I said that I for one knew this was no way for people to live and that it was costing countless innocent lives. Everybody cheered. I could see a few people were crying. After the speech, a few Palestinian New Yorkers and even a couple of Israelis came up to me and wanted to look at my head to see if they could make out any of their relatives. I let them. They didn't find who they were looking for. I was nervous the whole time that someone was going to fall out, and that it would be one of their relatives. Luckily, no one did. I got away as quickly as possible, and I told Kim that if I was going to do that anymore, I would need to know that no one was going to come inspect my head afterward.

That evening, Kim came home with me again. We wrote an ad together that she posted on like every Craigslist site in the world.

The next day, I had about two hundred new messages. None of them were from specialists who wanted to help me. They were all from journalists who wanted to interview me. The first interview I did was with the *Daily News*. I was on the cover the very next day. They called me "The Gazahawk Man."

I didn't even have a chance to see it for myself that morning before my mom called, totally going out of her mind. She insisted I come home right away. I thought it was better for her to see for herself that I was still alive and healthy. I took the train to Jersey and met her at home that afternoon.

She was waiting by the door when I walked up. She pushed me inside fast, I think before the neighbors would have a chance to see me, then she locked the door behind her and peeked out the window like maybe I was being followed. She sat me at the kitchen table and served me a bowl of the chicken soup she had already prepared. I reminded her I was a vegetarian. "Well maybe that's why this sort of thing keeps happening to you, Chelle," she said.

"What do you mean?" She insisted that I eat it. I took a couple slurps of the noodles and laid down the spoon. "Nothing like this has ever happened to me."

"Oh no?" She motioned to my flat chest.

"Mom! That's totally different. That was surgery. I chose that."

"I thought you said it *wasn't* a choice." She buttoned and unbuttoned the top of her shirt, like she does when she's upset. "Well, which is it? You can't have it both ways, Chelle."

I sighed and leaned back. "It's *Sheldon* now, Mom. Sheldon. Is that really so hard?"

"Oh no, no, no." She was starting to tear up and her voice was getting squeaky. "It's not hard. It's *easy*! It's always *sooo easy* with you, *Sheldon*."

"I didn't come here to fight, Mom."

"I know. I know. But this is really a lot, Chelle. You have to understand, this is a lot for me."

"It's a lot for me too, okay?"

She nodded, then wiped away a few little tears. "Do you really want to walk around with the Gaza Strip on your head for the rest of your life?" She stood and put more soup in my full bowl. "You really should think about this before you commit to it."

"Mom. God. I told you, this wasn't my choice."

"I know. I know." She sat the soup bowl down and waved her hands in the air. "I know we're all different in some ways. But first it was girls. And I said okay."

"Ummmmm, *no* you didn't."

"And then it was a different name and baggy jeans and I accepted that."

I rolled my eyes and groaned.

"Then it was the surgery. And Chelle, I just don't know. But now this. What am I supposed to do with *this*?" A series of pops started going off. I grimaced and sneezed as little flakes of dust rose and fell around my face. "Oh Lord, have mercy!" My mother jumped back and crossed herself. "Is that what happens when you get upset?"

"No, jeez. I don't know why I came here." I let out a long sigh. "Can I have a glass of milk? My throat's dry." She nodded and opened the fridge. "It's not me. It's Palestine and Israel, okay? I don't know if you know, but they're fighting right now."

She put the milk back in the fridge. "Don't patronize me, Sheldon. I know about Israel and Palestine. I keep up on current events too, you know."

She leaned down and handed me the glass of milk. As she did, her gaze was caught, and she stood, tilting her head and watching closely, little sounds coming from her, little "ohhh's" and "oh dear's." "Mmmmm. Well, would you look at that?" I sipped my milk and hunched my shoulders. Her eyes sparkled, transfixed as she watched. "Have you tried shampooing?" she asked in a whisper.

Two days later, I went on CNN. They actually paid me to be one of those talking heads (I guess that term has a new meaning for me) in the split-screen boxes. It's crazy how they do it. You're not actually in the room with anyone you're talking to. They just sit you in front of a screen, mic you, and put a little headphone in your ear. Then suddenly you hear a bunch of people who are also on the screen in front of you shouting in your ear. It was really awful for me, because their shouting was competing with the ruckus on my head.

The interview consisted of me, a rabbi, an Israeli spokeswoman, a male Palestinian professor living in the US, and a Barbie-blond female moderator. When the sound came on they were all in the middle of shouting at each other. The Palestinian professor was pounding his fist, saying that Israel fired first and broke the treaty. The Israeli spokeswoman shouted back, very flustered, her sentences breaking. "If Israel hadn't started firing first in this case . . . you know, Israel had security reasons. There is no deal not to retaliate. Israel always reserves the right to go in and attack if there are real security breaches, and there were."

The Palestinian shouted, "What are the breaches that merit this level of response?"

The spokeswoman became breathlessly upset. "Hezbollah has been firing rockets for several weeks into Israel! And we believe a team of Hamas fighters were digging a tunnel to kidnap Israeli soldiers."

"AND YOU ASSASSINATED THEM!" the Palestinian professor hollered back. "You have not even any proof that is what they were doing! It was a tunnel for smuggling *food. They were smuggling FOOD!*"

"Okay, okay," the moderator interrupted. "We are being joined now by a special guest, Sheldon Peters, also known as the Gazahawk Man. Mr. Peters, maybe you can help us clear some things up. Yours is a very exceptional situation. For those of you who don't know, what seems to be a flesh-and-blood animated replica of a section of the Gaza Strip has grown on your head. Is that correct?"

"Yes. That's right."

"Can we get a close-up on that, Larry?"

The camera zoomed in, cutting away from the other guests, and I saw, magnified on the screen, the wall, the people, the houses and trees, and all the things happening in the little world on my head. The camera pulled back. All the guests were squinting dumbfounded into their screens. The Barbie moderator was still smiling, unfazed. "Which section, exactly, of the barrier wall were we just looking at?"

"Well. I'm not sure *exactly*, but I've been told it's definitely on the Palestine-Israel border, and I think it's somewhere near the town of Kahna."

"Why is that?"

"Well, because it's a stone section, not the wire fence, and also some of the recent events in that area sync up with what has been happening on my head."

"So the events in this section of the barrier happen in real time on your head?"

"Yes, that seems to be the case."

"So maybe you can tell us once and for all," the moderator continued, "who fired first?"

"This is irrelevant," the rabbi shouted, waving his arms. "This is not a political matter. This is a personal, spiritual phenomenon!"

I held my hand up. "I don't know. It didn't happen until two days after the siege started."

Everyone except the moderator nodded and looked relieved. She leaned in and clasped her hands in front of her. She seemed to shine with clean white makeup and polished hair. "Can you speak just from your personal experience, Mr. Peters, and tell us who you *feel* is at fault here?"

"This is ridiculous," the Israeli spokeswoman said, leaning back and almost laughing. "One person's experience of having the Gaza Strip on his head for a couple of weeks cannot define centuries of history and struggle."

"I have to agree with her there," the Palestinian professor interjected.

"Well I'm glad you two can finally agree on something. But it's Mr. Peters's turn to speak and I think the world is interested in hearing his side." The moderator nodded to me, "Please go on, Mr. Peters."

"Well, I don't know who's to blame, but I know it's definitely much more itchy on the Palestinian side of my head."

"What does that mean, it's itchy?" the rabbi asked.

"It's more itchy because there are a lot more people in a very small space. And mostly all the gunshots and bombs are on that side, I mean, landing on that side, you know. Like, all the bombs are going to that side."

"Is it affecting your health?" the moderator asked. "Do you think you have any symptoms of traumatic stress disorder?"

"I . . . I don't know."

"The fact is, on the twenty-fifth, Israel fired fifty missiles into Palestine," the professor said, leaning in. "Mr. Peters, can you account for disparities in casualties?"

"Oh yes. There was a cluster bomb fired into Palestine the other night. I felt that. And there were at least twelve casualties from it."

"You see!" the professor continued. "And how many casualties from Palestine total have you . . . experienced?"

"It's hard to say. More than sixty."

"Just on this section of the barrier, and just in a matter of weeks!" he went on. "And Mr. Peters, how many Israeli casualties have you experienced?"

"Two. They both appeared to be soldiers."

"The fact that there aren't casualties in Israel shouldn't be held against us," the spokeswoman said emphatically. "There are thousands of Israelis living in bomb shelters all over Israel right now. We're being held hostage in our own homes. It doesn't speak against us that more of us aren't dying, does it?" She was completely outraged with me.

"Mr. Peters, do you have any knowledge of the tunnel that was allegedly dug from Palestine into Israel?" the moderator asked.

"No. It's only what's happening above ground . . . on my head."

The moderator tapped her pen thoughtfully.

"I have a question for him," the rabbi said. "How can you be sure of the exact number of casualties and if they are soldiers? It appears very small." He squinted toward the screen. "It would be hard to know for certain, wouldn't it? Where are you getting this estimate?"

"That's a good point. It's very small. It would be difficult to count the number of dead or wounded without a magnifying glass. Do you check and watch it closely every day?" the professor asked.

"No. Ummmm. No. Not exactly."

"You see. There's no way to justify his statements," the rabbi said, waving his hand as if swatting a fly from the room.

"No ... It's not like that," I said softly, my voice cracking.

"I'm sorry, Mr. Peters. You're going to have to speak up," the moderator told me. "It's not like what?"

Everybody waited. "It's ... well." My mouth felt dry. I swallowed hard and went on. "I know the number for sure because, when they die, see ..." It was hard to say.

"Yes, go on."

"When they die, they ... they fall out. They fall off my head. The bodies, when they're dead, they fall."

For the first time everyone was completely silent. The moderator didn't look so shiny right then. "Ohhhhhhh," she whispered. The Palestinian professor swallowed hard and nodded. The other two sat very still. The moderator regained her glistening smile, turned to the camera, and segued into a commercial break.

I did a couple more interviews like that, acting as a commentator. I didn't like it, but the money was good. I was also asked to go on these daytime talk shows. The only one I said yes to was *Oprah*. I was getting kind of tired of the exposure, but who says no to *Oprah*? I had always thought if I was on *Oprah*, or doing TV interviews, it would be to talk about being trans. In a way, this has helped with that. Now, the last thing on anyone's mind is my gender. I'm just a man. That's like one of the least interesting things about me. Even Oprah only brought it up for a second. It was like, "So, Sheldon isn't your original name, is it? You were born a woman, and you transgendered. Is that the right term? Okay. And one day recently, you woke up with the

Gaza Strip on your head? Is that right?" And that's all she really said about it.

In the middle of the second month, the whole thing was driving me crazy. I hadn't yet learned to live with it like I have now. The fighting was still pretty intense. I felt desperate for some peace, so I went on the news one last time and made a statement that I wished to meet with the president in person. He said yes. I guess it was a good PR move. I actually got a ten-minute meeting with him in private. I thought maybe I could show him the direness of the situation.

Kim prepped me before the meeting. I hadn't been sure what to ask for, but we decided that I was going to ask that he stop funding the Israeli military. I took a very special gift for him that I kept tucked in my shirt pocket.

I couldn't get through the metal detector without it beeping, obviously, so they patted me down and metal-detected me all over with a handheld device. Four Secret Service officers led me into the Oval Office. The president stood and shook my hand. He directed me to sit in the chair across from his desk. The presidential seal is really intimidating, and whether you want to be or not, you can't help but be intimidated by the president. Kim had warned me, "Don't let him intimidate you," so I tried to push through it. Luckily, he was obviously intimidated by me too. That day, there was a lot of machine gun fire on my head, and even though he's always really cool, I could make out his right eyebrow twitching each time the sound of little pops emanated from my neckline. "That's near the checkpoint," I told him. "There are some activists there today hammering at the wall."

"I see. Yours is a very exceptional situation," he told me. He's a very earnest man, not only on television, but even in person. His calm, earnest manner seems very sincere, but there is something infuriatingly impenetrable about it as well. "I just want to start by expressing my deep sorrow that a civilian has had to experience these types of . . . upheavals."

"You mean an *American* civilian." I was proud of myself for starting strong, like Kim said to do.

"Look, let me be clear." He knocked on his desk. "I do not support the level of the recent retaliation of the Israeli government. I condemn the killing of innocent civilians. I am doing everything in my power to ensure that peace has a chance to re-emerge."

"Then are you going to defund the Israeli military, at least momentarily? Can you make sure that US money isn't going toward weapons like cluster bombs?" Sure, Kim had coached me a little, but I meant it. This was my only chance to talk to someone who might be able to give me some peace finally.

I don't remember exactly what he said then, because he talked for several minutes. He said something about Gandhi being a good man, and that he was trying to continue to foster a nation where people like Gandhi could exist, and he loved Gandhi, but he's not Gandhi, he's the president of the United States, and the issues are complex.

I was very frustrated by the whole thing. I told him that I wasn't going to pay my taxes until the US stopped providing the weapons that were being fired on *my* head.

He told me again that mine was obviously an exceptional situation and that he wasn't quite sure what the legal implications were, but that I would most likely still face an audit if I chose to do that.

I stood up and bent down, shaking my head and pointing to it.

"You would find a way to stop this if you were me," I shouted. "This should have happened to you, not me. This is on your head more than mine." He leaned back, clasping his hands in front of him.

A Secret Service officer stepped up and took hold of my shoulder. "Sir, you're going to have to calm down or I will remove you."

The president lifted his hand. "It's okay," he said. "I can understand why you are so upset." We stared at each other for a second, not saying anything.

I turned to the Secret Service officer. "I have something to give him, okay? I'm going to get it out of my shirt pocket now." I didn't want them to think I was pulling out a weapon. "Mr. President, I have something for you." My mouth went dry as I reached into my front pocket. The Secret Service guy was watching very carefully, standing shoulder to shoulder with me. I held out my cupped hand. "I hope you'll take her, and keep her as a reminder." The president looked from the officer to me, wonder crossing his face. I waited. He held out his open palm below mine. I dropped her in. It wasn't a bomb, but it almost might as well have been. Amazing how something so tiny can have such an effect. But I guess a corpse is a corpse, no matter how small.

His hand trembled as he cradled her. His mouth fell open and his face paled. He slumped. The Secret Service officers did not react, but I saw one them looking. "Who is she?"

"I don't know. She's just a kid who fell out of my head a few days ago. I don't know her name."

"Thank you, Mr. Peters, for illuminating the full weight of your situation. I appreciate it." He nodded at the officer next to me. "Would you please show Mr. Peters to the lawn."

I was escorted out. Twenty minutes later I met the president on the lawn. The press took pictures of us shaking hands. The headlines read GAZAHAWK MAN AND PREZ TALK PEACE.

That's it. It's been more than a year now. Nothing has really changed. I got some gallery offers. Maybe I'll do a show. Only, I haven't produced any new work for a while. Somehow I have a feeling that won't matter. It's not about the work anyway. Now I'm known, I have a name, a public identity.

My mom sends me new shampoos every week. Kim still comes around. But we're just friends. I think she's more intrigued by my head than she is by me. Mostly, I keep to myself. I spend a lot of time looking in the mirror. Maybe I'll start sketching some self-portraits. I always thought that kind of thing was indulgent, but now I'm more than myself. Maybe I always was. I can do sketches close up and far away. It wouldn't just be me I was sketching. It's all there, on me, part of me, falling from me.

REVELATIONS

"This word from the Lord has come to us. It has come as a gift, and we shouldn't fear it."

"No, we won't fear it," was repeated in murmurs, which spread through the small congregation. Sarah sat in the fourth pew from the front, her Bible resting open on her lap. She shook her head no, along with the rest of them, and clenched her hands, looking solemnly forward as Pastor Rick continued.

"Now, this word has come to us because therein lies something we must learn. And this is greater than us, as men with men's intellects, can know by our own means and ways. My wife, Tracy," the pastor gestured to his wife, who sat in the front pew, "has received tidings from her prayers before. When she came to me, I prayed upon it, and the Lord told to me as well that, indeed, what she is said be the truth." The pastor was an uneducated man in his late fifties who had been raised on a farm, and began preaching at local churches just out of high school. When he stood at the pulpit, he spoke more formally than was natural for him, but which he felt was most befitting of a pastor. The result was an awkward combination of rural colloquia and grammatically incorrect, albeit somewhat biblical-sounding English. "And I hope you all will pray upon this matter also, as we have, and therefore come to know what for it is that we have come to know we must come to find it out."

Sarah *had* prayed on it, and she feared it was her they were seeking to find out. God didn't speak so clearly to her as He did to her pastor and his wife. For her, God was a voice that came from a distance, through a thick fog, and it was difficult to differentiate His voice from her own. It was difficult to be sure that she wasn't talking to herself. And therein lay the horrible evidence of her sinful heart. It was her confident, boasting nature, she thought, that even now, at the age of seventy-three, was her ultimate downfall, and God help her, possibly even the downfall of the entire congregation. It was her love of herself, her vain and willful arrogance that had led to this.

Edmund raised his hand and stood. "Brother Rick, I have a testimony," he bellowed. Edmund stood large, his broad stomach leading the way through his blue jean overalls and red flannel shirt, some version of which he was always wearing. He had been a cow farmer his entire life, and had come to the church ten years ago at the age of thirty-seven after his wife left him and took the children due to repeated bouts of rage brought on by years of angry drinking. "I've prayed on this as well, all week since Sunday when you first told us what your wife had heard from God. And through prayer, I also know what you said is true, though the Lord hasn't yet seen fit to show me where this . . ." he searched for words, "darkness lies, or what form it's taken. I also think you're right. It's in one of us, and we got to stamp it out."

"Amen," Betty said softly, followed by Tracy and Rick.

Pastor Rick held up his hand. "Now this is a blessing, so let's not speak of this as a stamping out. This darkness that the Lord has shown us is here amongst us, and it could be residing within any one of us." Sarah's eyes scanned the congregation. The others were looking at one another as well. Rick placed his hand over his chest. "Edmund, this might come as a shock, but be not yourself surprised to think, it could be *me*, for all we know. I'm not free of sin. It could be you. Remember, 'for all have sinned and fallen short of the glory of God.' We should not speak of this as a stamping out. Whomever it is harbors this darkness, they'll need our help to shed it. They are one of us, and remember, 'there but for grace go I.'"

"You're right. You're right. I'm sorry," Edmund said, resuming his seat.

"No harm, brother." Rick looked to his congregation. "Has anyone else testimony upon this matter? Have you all prayed upon it? Has the Lord shown you anything, anything you would like to share with us here today?" Two hands went up, then a third, then two more, then all the hands were raised except Sarah's. Then Sarah raised her hand as well.

Just four days prior to this evening's service, Rick preached a sermon that had deeply affected every member of the congregation. His wife, Tracy, had, for the third time since she and her husband had come to the church, received a divine message from the Lord. This time, the Lord had revealed to her the reason that the congregation had been so steadily dwindling in numbers over the last three years, from an average of eighty members on Sunday mornings, to a low thirty, and now, in the third year of its decline, the congregation was made up of little more than a consistent and devoted fifteen people, three of which, including Sarah, were the church's founding members who had, in the mid-seventies, helped build the very building which still housed the congregation.

The message from the Lord was exacting: Some member (or perhaps even *members*) of the congregation was housing within their heart, maybe their very soul, a darkness, the precise nature of which the Lord did not reveal. But it was, the Lord had said, a darkness the person was not willing to admit even to themselves was evil, and therefore, they could not be relieved of it. This darkness was poisoning their lives, and preventing the Lord from blessing the congregation. Indeed, this darkness was the reason so many members, over the last few years, had either backslidden or abandoned the congregation for unspoken reasons. This is what their pastor had told them. This is what they had been called to pray on. They were all called to pray to the Lord to let them know if this word Tracy had received was true, and to begin searching themselves for traces of such a dark thing residing within them.

Many had searched themselves, with great fear of what insidious thing they might find plaguing their minds. Sarah had searched herself, and she'd found, very quickly, a thing within herself that could be such a dark thing. But she was loath to fully believe that this thing was horrible enough to cause the Lord to descend from on high and tell Tracy that it needed to be blotted out.

"As we leave tonight, I want you to take this with you," Rick preached. He opened his Bible and began to read from the pages he'd marked with yellow Post-it notes. "He who conceals his transgressions will not prosper, but he who confesses and forsakes them will find compassion. Proverbs ... You have placed our iniquities before You," he boomed. "Our secret sins shine in the light of Your presence." He raised the Bible above his head and shook it. "Who can discern his errors? Acquit me of hidden faults." He slammed it to the pulpit. "People, let us come and pray together." They bowed their heads and recited the prayer they all knew so well, ending the evening's service.

The air outside was cold and sweet. Headlights shone against the white church door where Rick and Tracy stood bidding their farewells as the members departed.

Betty approached Sarah, who was parked at the far end of the church drive, as she was opening her car door. "One minute, Sarah." She waved as she approached.

"Well, hello there," Sarah said sweetly, turning to greet her friend.

"How are you?"

"Oh, I can't complain. You?"

"Well," Betty placed her hand on Sarah's wrist and sighed. "This has been quite a week." Sarah nodded in agreement. "I would love to get together and pick your brain about all of this."

"I honestly don't know what to think," Sarah said, shifting her purse on her shoulder and shaking her head.

"It really *is* a lot to take in, isn't it?" Betty asked. The two women had known each other since they were much younger. A woman of sixty-eight, Betty had come to the church just a few years after it was opened, and they'd been casual friends for most of their lives.

Sarah pressed a strand of her long, silver hair behind her ear. "Like I said, I don't know. There's obviously *something* going wrong. We've been losing people left and right, and Tracy has received word from the Lord before. However much we might wish otherwise, she's always been right."

Betty agreed. "Surely. Jacob Hollimeister, you mean?"

"Well yes. She was right about him. No arguing that."

"When she saw the demon of homosexuality on that boy? Oh dear."

Sarah nodded. "That poor boy."

Betty looked side to side, checking that there was no one within earshot. "Yes, but can I just say, it didn't exactly take a psychic to see that, if you know what I mean. She may have had a word from the Lord, but anyway, it wasn't a very well-disguised demon." Sarah giggled and Betty giggled harder. The women quickly covered their mouths to quiet themselves.

"We shouldn't joke," Sarah told her, trying to regain an air of seriousness. "He has to live with it, probably the rest of his life. His parents even, they're enabling him now, and they don't have anyone to support them since they left the church."

"Oh, I know. I know." Betty patted her arm. "It's a new world out there." She shook her head. "Anyway, Ellen and I were hoping you'd have lunch with us tomorrow, so we can talk about all this, and you know, commiserate."

"Well," Sarah looked around at the nearly empty drive and the few remaining members saying their goodbyes and getting in their cars, "I suppose that would be fine."

"My house at noon, then. I'll make some lunch for everyone, and maybe, would you mind bringing something for dessert?"

Sarah smiled politely. She placed her keys in the car door. "That sounds just fine." Over Betty's shoulder, she saw Pastor Rick watching them. He raised his hand and waved. Sarah waved back. Betty turned and waved farewell to the pastor and his wife, smiling sweetly. The pastor hollered Betty's name, and motioned for her to come over. She nodded and shouted that she would be right there. "All right, I'll go see what he wants now. It's probably about the cleaning schedule," she told Sarah. They hugged lightly, and departed.

Sarah's large house had felt lonely to her for the last few years, since her husband died. She was the oldest of four children, and she'd helped her mother raise her three siblings, until she got married at seventeen. She'd had three children of her own, all of whom had long since grown and moved away. And when her husband died, she found herself living alone for the first time in her life at the age of seventy. This wasn't an age at which she'd foreseen herself having to adapt to such unfamiliar circumstances. When she'd thought of beginning a new chapter at this stage of life, she'd always pictured her husband there with her. She'd always pictured herself becoming more dependent.

The large house sat at the front of a full acre of land, which she was now charged with keeping up. Every time she walked up to the house alone, and thought of the emptiness that awaited her in those large rooms, it was hard for her to enter it. Once she was inside it was all right, but entering the house was always difficult to do alone. She couldn't help feeling astonished each time that her husband was not sitting in his chair beside the love seat, waiting for her, sipping his coffee and watching the news, or asleep behind the paper.

She made her way up the sidewalk, but when she got to the house she stopped, turned around, and sat down on the porch, taking a moment to enjoy the fresh, cool air and get a look at the stars.

The stars were brilliant out in the country, as there were no nearby cities to obscure their light. The ravens rustled in the trees above her. She would feed them in the morning, scattering bread and birdseed on the lawn, and enjoy the sight of their shining black wings coming down to collect their little treats. When she was younger, it had been sparrows, robins, and two cardinals. Then, more recently, the ravens had taken over, and chased all the other birds away. Many people didn't, but she preferred them. She thought they looked regal and dignified, and she knew they were supposedly the most intelligent of wild birds in the area. They kept her company. She felt that she and the ravens had a real understanding, and she didn't mind that her popularity with the ravens gave her a touch of eccentricity, making her a bit more mysterious, a bit more interesting to the other members of her small town.

In the spaces between the branches of early autumn, she had a good view of the clear night sky. She spotted Cassiopeia, and enjoyed its light. She tried to see the old woman in the rocking chair, and although she knew what it was supposed to be, it always just looked like a very beautifully crafted *W* to her. A breeze came up, and a shudder ran through her as she recalled the darkness she was supposed to be searching herself for, which she'd found so easily and without much digging. It had to do with the thing she was about to do, but was much more than that thing as well.

She picked up her purse and stood, entering the house and turning on the kitchen light, immediately looking to the dim living room where her husband of more than fifty years no longer sat. A deep sadness forced its way toward her, but she shoved it off and went into the bathroom where she washed her face and took a brush to her long, silken gray hair.

She undressed and regarded herself in the mirror. Her naked body defied her. A part of her loathed how wrinkled and foreign her skin had become with age, but it was the part that didn't find this altogether distasteful that caused her the most upset. Unlike her face and hands, which had remained smooth and gave her the appearance of someone much more youthful than was usual for a woman her age, the skin on her belly, neck, and hips was wrinkled, and strange to her, that of an old woman. Even more startling, though, was that she still had a lovely woman's shape, and her breasts had remained full, taut and smooth. Her breasts, her face, her hands and arms, were smooth and pale, and appeared young. She didn't know whether to be repelled by or happy with her body. When she looked at herself, a feeling that she now worried was a darkness swept over her. She felt sensual, not in spite of, but with her wrinkles and all. She saw that she was older, and parts of her had worn and changed, but she also saw that there was something about this body that could be desired. It might be desired in an altogether different way than it was before, but with no less ferocity. Her husband had desired her until the end of his life. She was a beautiful woman at twenty-three and she was a beautiful woman at seventy-three. She'd always been complimented on her striking appearance: her high cheekbones, and full lips, and sharp, severe eyes, framed by a mane of hair that once was a deep brunette, and had now turned into a brilliant collection of silvery gray and white streaks hanging down well past her shoulders. She stood naked in front of the mirror, looking at her own body and enjoying the fact that men would no doubt still desire her. Her house was not the only thing that had been left empty when her husband died.

Her fingers clasped nothing, missing the feeling of his interlocking, and her lips had gone unkissed, and in her chest she felt a lonesomeness and need that was growing so great she didn't know if it would ever be possible to fill it again. She remembered the feel of his long body against hers; her head pressed against the flatness of his chest, and his slender hands sliding along her hips, taking her by the chin, and kissing her deeply, as he always had, with sweetness and desire all mingling.

What she wanted to do, what she had been doing, she realized, was awful. Each night before bed, she stood in front of the mirror and imagined him, her dead husband, making love to her, and she touched herself until she was satisfied. And then she would sometimes cry quietly, and then she would go to bed.

Defiling herself to a dead man's image. What could she have been thinking? What could be more horrible? Of course she always knew, somewhere in her, she knew without a doubt that this was wrong, but she was so conceited and selfish, she wouldn't allow herself to admit it. Years she'd been doing this now, and what's worse, it had evolved. It wasn't always her husband in her thoughts. Images of other men came into her mind as well: men she didn't know, men who very well might not even exist; men whose bodies and temperaments she created perfect, solely to satisfy her own lust. They would come into her mind and she welcomed the images of them because the thought of them didn't fill her with grief like the thought of her dead husband did. She could experience pleasure alone with these false men. Pleasure not found around anything, beyond anything;

without having to sneak pleasure around the sadness or darkness of her grief.

Without this satisfaction, she had nearly only grief when she was alone and nothing to keep it at bay. She believed deeply that her husband was awaiting her in heaven, and when her time came she would rejoin him there, not as husband and wife, but as brother and sister living their days together in the Lord's light and eternal grace. Beyond this deeply held belief, though, was a deeper fear that none of it was true. She'd always been a religious woman, and a woman of strong conviction. At the same time, she questioned, privately and silently. Since she was young, she'd believed. But also, she'd questioned, and when her husband died, it was like someone had struck her in the face with the knuckled back of a strong hand made of nothing but that question. When she thought of death, of his absence from the remainder of her life, and her own inevitable death, like the pointed end of a needle whose true usefulness she'd never fully grasped, she felt as cold as a distant star looks: sparkling and white hovering in darkness, blinking and blind, the weight of the void its only tether. Her private, nightly pleasure staved off these thoughts when she was alone, and gave her something, however small, to look forward to each day.

Still, this was no excuse for such a grotesque act. A woman her age, pleasuring herself to the thought of a dead man, to her husband, yes, but also, to other men; many other men. It was too horrible to admit. How would she? *Would* she confess it? Was this the thing that the Lord had sent word about? Of course it was. What could be worse? It was depraved. How could she tell a pastor such a thing, even if to beg forgiveness? She couldn't bear the thought.

Although she knew it was wrong, and that it was a thing for

which she must seek repentance, even now, she wanted terribly to lean back against the wall and place her hand on herself and feel some release, some sense of fulfillment again, even if it was only once more. *But isn't that what addicts say: just one more time?* she thought.

She splashed water on her face, then grudgingly slipped into her robe. She hung her head, went and sat on her bed and began to weep. She tried to pray, but as often happened she could hear no other voice besides her own when she tried. God was not speaking to her, not tonight. And she didn't know if it was because of this awful thing she'd made a practice of, or because of something she feared too greatly to give much credence to. Whether He spoke back or not, she decided He must be listening, so she repented and asked Him for help overcoming her depravity. These prayers only took her to crying harder, and soon she had exhausted herself. She climbed up and curled in the bed, quickly falling into a fatigued and troubled sleep.

She woke at seven in the morning quite naturally, and went about toasting bread and boiling one egg, which she took with black tea as her breakfast. Then she showered and dressed while the morning news played on the radio. After this, she threw on a light jacket and took a small paper bag of birdseed into her front yard, and the ravens descended about her, enjoying the daily offering. As the birds pecked at the seeds in the grass, she pondered what she would do. She hoped this lunch meeting with Betty and Ellen would strengthen her resolve in some way, and give her some clearer notion how to move forward. Should she confess, she wondered, would the pastor keep the nature of her transgression private, or would it have to be revealed to the congregation? If it was revealed, she thought, she wouldn't be able to bear it. Or perhaps this was all silly. Perhaps Tracy was a silly woman who misunderstood things, and she was creating a drama where there was nothing truly sinister beyond everyday human transgressions. Sarah suddenly became very angry at the whole situation, and wished it would just go away, that someone else would come forward with something much worse than anything she had to hide, or that the congregation would forget the whole event entirely, and they could move forward with things as they were. It was a small congregation, but it was enough for her. They had the Easter revival, which brought five Baptist churches from the county together each year, and the Fifth Sunday Potlucks, and the Summer Children's Bible School, and what was wrong with it? She let out a frustrated sigh and dumped the remainder of the birdseed in a pile on the ground, causing the crows to caw and fight as she went back into the house, slamming the door for no one to hear.

On the way to Betty's house, she stopped by the local grocery store and picked up a lemon cake for dessert, which Betty thanked her for when she came in the door, taking the cake from her and displaying it on the center of the dining room table. "Look what Sarah brought us," she told Ellen, who sat on the opposite side of the table, sipping tea from a little blue and white floral-pattern china cup, next to Frank, whom Sarah had not expected to see.

"Well, hello, Frank. I didn't know you were coming today." He stood as Sarah took a seat at the table.

"I hope you don't mind my being here. We've all been talking about this," he paused, "and *praying* on it, and, well, I just wanted to add my two cents and catch up with you lovely ladies."

"Of course," Sarah said. "So nice to see you." She knew she wouldn't be able to speak candidly about her fears with a man present. Frank was a widower, like herself, but was widowed many years prior, and unlike her, being single seemed to suit him. He was a well-built man in his late sixties who always kept himself up nicely, dressing in collared shirts and tailored slacks, his salt-and-pepper-colored hair combed and sprayed stiffly to the side. He was quite a handsome, charming man and had done well in life. He had a very nice house on the edge of town and was fairly wealthy, having retired early after designing a piece of a machine that was used in car parts factories around the world. He'd explained the thing to Sarah several times over the years, and she never quite understood exactly what this thing he'd designed was or did, except that this thing was very mechanically versatile, and it sold well enough that he didn't have to worry about money anymore.

"Ellen, how are you? How's Wayne? Is he coming, too?" she asked.

"Oh, you know, he's watching his games. He didn't feel like coming this afternoon," she said of her husband, and pushed the honey toward Sarah. "For your tea?"

"Oh yes, thank you." Sarah noticed the air in the house smelled of something good, but unfamiliar. "What kind of potpourri is that?" she asked.

"Oh, it's not a potpourri," Betty told her. "It's actually an incense. Frank got me hooked on the stuff since his trip to India."

"Well, it smells wonderful," Sarah said. "Incense. My goodness."

Betty went around the table setting tuna sandwiches and chips in front of her three guests and finally took a seat by Sarah.

"Thanks, this looks terrific," Frank told her, picking up his sandwich and taking a large bite. "Mmmm, delicious."

"Thank you for making us lunch, Betty," Ellen told her politely, before turning her attention back to Sarah. "You know, honestly, I don't think Wayne is really taking this stuff with Tracy very seriously."

"Not everyone *is* taking it seriously!" Frank snapped, laying his sandwich down and smacking his lips.

There was a long silence after this statement and Sarah chewed her sandwich noticing that everyone at the table was watching her, waiting for a response. "Is that right?" she asked pleasantly, trying not to show judgment one way or another.

"Well now," Betty said, nodding to Frank, "that's exactly why we're here, isn't it?"

Sarah nodded and took a sip of her tea. "It's good tea. What is it?"

"Vanilla chai," Betty answered, and smiled tensely, pursing her lips. There was another uncomfortable silence where everyone but Frank tried to look pleasantly at one another. The women ate more of their sandwiches.

Frank tapped his finger on the table in deep thought. Finally he let out, "May we talk candidly with you, Sarah?"

She was a bit taken aback by his tone, and also at the "we," which seemed to imply these three were of one mind, perhaps had even spoken of the subject they were about to embark on previously, and she was the odd person out. "Well, of course," Sarah told him. "Why wouldn't you?"

"Good," Frank nodded and continued. "Not everyone in the church is happy with the way Rick and Tracy have been handling things the last few years. These words from the Lord she receives, well, sometimes they seem like little more, I'm saying, to some people, they seem like little more than veiled accusations."

"It's not Christ-like to accuse," Ellen said in a sweet singsong tone. As she interjected, she moved her hand across the table toward Frank, who took it up and patted the top of it tenderly.

"I couldn't agree more, sister," he told her. "It's undignified." Ellen smiled back at him.

Ellen was a roundish, short woman in her late fifties who worked part-time as a secretary at the county hospital. Sarah had never known that Ellen and Frank were so friendly with each other. She knew Frank was not a friend of Wayne's, Ellen's husband. They were very different types of men. Her husband, Wayne, was a retired truck driver who still did odd jobs, mostly in home repair. Ellen had always been very active in the church, but her husband only attended the Sunday morning services occasionally, and one could tell he only attended because his wife was dragging him along.

"Maybe it is a word from God," Betty said, lifting her tea glass and stirring in some cream. She smiled at Sarah. Of everyone, she was closest to Betty, who was nearest her own age and had been her friend for many, many years. "But, also, maybe she's confused. There's really no way to know. I'll admit, I've prayed on it, and I haven't received a clear answer." She shook her head and looked up toward the ceiling, in thought. "The Lord doesn't speak to me so clearly. I feel His presence, but I don't hear those types of messages, except once." Sarah sighed, relieved to hear this. Betty continued, "Years ago, when my sister died, God came to me the day before and told me that it was time to call her and to apologize for something I'd done to her years before that had caused an argument, and that I'd always felt very guilty for. And I did. And the next day, she died in a car wreck, you probably remember. But I never told you this, the moment it happened, I knew. I was just sitting at home alone, and suddenly, I knew she was dead. I could feel it in my bones."

"I've heard of other people who've received those kinds of messages when their loved ones passed," Ellen said.

"But other than that," Betty went on, "I don't get such clear messages from God. I hope it doesn't mean I'm a bad Christian."

"Not at all." Sarah couldn't help herself. She was overcome. "I feel the same way. I don't hear Him clearly, either."

"Well, that's good to know. No one would question *your* faith," Betty told her.

"When I pray," Sarah admitted, "especially since my husband died, I have so much time to myself, and sometimes it's difficult to tell whose voice it is, God's, or my own mind. Is that awful?"

They all paused and looked at Sarah, turning over what she'd said. "So, you do hear a voice, you just don't know if it's God's? Is that what you mean?" Frank inquired. Sarah felt a chill come over her. She'd said too much. She was already giving herself away.

"Do you ever wonder if, perhaps, it's not God's voice, but not your own, either?"

"What? No. What do you mean? Whose voice would it be?" Sarah was taken aback.

"Oh, I don't know." Ellen shrugged. "There are many other entities, demonic and angelic, that could, hypothetically, come to us. You've never thought of that?"

Sarah blanched. "Well, no. I know that the Devil is a master of disguise. But, I always thought, if a thing like that ever happened to me, well I . . . I don't know . . . I would just . . ."

Betty touched Sarah's arm. "We're getting off track here. Sarah, what do you think about all this business with the church? We haven't even asked you."

Sarah took a breath, and looked around the table. "Well, I don't know. To be candid with you, I've worried it could even," she took a deep breath, "it could be me, harboring this," she paused and took another breath, "horrible thing."

"Nonsense!" Ellen said. "You? Nonsense."

Sarah held up her hand. "Remember, none of us is perfect. And I do worry. Since my husband died, I've sometimes been so lonely." Her voice quivered but she pressed on. "I do wonder if I'm... wallowing in my own pain, allowing my thoughts to become too dark, and not allowing God to lead me out of it. And worse," this was hardest for her to say without revealing too much, "I have a greedy heart and want more out of the time I have left, and after I have already lived so fully and been so blessed."

"Sarah," Ellen said pointedly, "grieving for your husband is not a sin."

"It's only natural," Frank told her, "for a woman as youthful, full of life, and beautiful," Sarah blushed, "as yourself to feel lonely sometimes. Why, I can't tell you how I felt after I lost Marie. But this isn't something to be repentant of."

"You're still alive. *You* didn't die," Betty told her.

Sarah brushed her hair behind her ear nervously. "Maybe I'm just being overanxious, but if there is something sinful, something dark residing in our congregation, of course, it would be best to remove it. It's just that I also worry that this type of thing... the way they are going about it, might do more harm than good." The others nodded in agreement. "I worry this, whatever it is, could further divide us and, I don't know, run another person off or cause them to be shunned, and we don't need to lose any more people. Perhaps, even if Tracy is right, it should be handled with more..." she searched for words, "discretion?"

"We are of the same mind," Frank boomed.

"Although," Sarah went on, "Tracy has been right before. I would just, honestly, yes, like to see it handled differently."

"What does she mean? When was she right?" Frank asked the other two women.

Ellen had a mouthful of chips. She spoke through the crunching. "With that little gay boy, and that young couple, Sam and Andrea. You remember."

"Gay boy? You mean Jacob?" he asked.

"Yes," Betty nodded.

"I remember! That was handled atrociously." Frank swallowed a bite of his sandwich. "He's a good kid, and he's doing quite well for himself anyway. Just got a scholarship for engineering," Frank said.

"You still speak to him?" Sarah asked.

"Only on *occasion*," Betty said, pinching up her face into a weird smile and shaking her head. She held her teacup on a tiny plate against her chest. She took a quick sip again.

"And the young couple," Ellen went on. "They weren't married and they had just moved in together, and after Tracy spoke about her prayers, oh it was a scene. You remember? Rick preached the whole sermon on fornication, and they never came back again. And two other young couples left shortly after that, too." Ellen placed her napkin in her lap. "Andrea's still very upset about the whole ordeal."

"You still speak to them, too?" Sarah asked.

"Only on *occasion*!" Betty told her again, more loudly this time, shaking her head quickly. She laughed nervously. "We've all bumped into them here and there. It's a small town."

"Well, I've never seen them again," Sarah said.

"I have," Ellen said quickly, "at the grocery store and a few other places. And, you know, I don't think they're so bad. Young people, they don't all get married right away these days."

"This is what I mean." Frank clenched his fists. "The world is evolving. We have to evolve with it. It's not the 1950s anymore. We've lost all the young folks, and there's a reason for it, and it very well may not lie within the congregation, but I think, honestly, it may have to do with the leadership."

"So, the three of you don't believe Tracy?" Sarah asked, feeling astonished at everything she'd heard, but also relieved by the thought that her secret may not be as horrible a sin as she'd talked herself into believing it was.

"I for one don't give it any credence, and if I were you, I wouldn't tell them anything about the voices you hear, or who knows, they might burn you at the stake." Frank was turning red in the face.

Sarah was shocked by his outburst. Betty touched his elbow. "Calm down now. We're all friends here. It's not that bad." She turned to Sarah. "I don't feel as strongly as Frank does. I'm not sure. I don't think Tracy is lying, per se. Just mistaken. Of course, she may well have heard a word from the Lord. There may be someone harboring some awful sin, some 'darkness' as she said, which they need to disabuse themselves of. That's very possible. I just wish it would be handled differently. And we've asked you here because, well, we've been meaning to talk to you for a while. We just weren't sure how you would feel about all this."

Ellen stirred her tea. "We're not the only ones, you know?" she told Sarah.

"The only ones, what?" Sarah asked, confused.

Betty raised an eyebrow at Ellen and scratched her chin. "Don't you think we're getting ahead of ourselves a bit, darling?"

"Look," Frank said to Sarah, "can you assure me that this is all going to be kept between just us? We'll offer you the same discretion with what you've shared as well, in regards to the voices and all."

"I never said I heard voices *exactly*, I just—"

Frank cut Sarah off. "All I'm saying is, it's a delicate matter, and until we are sure how we're actually going to proceed, I think our discussions are best kept private."

Sarah shrugged. "Certainly."

"We have your word?"

"Well, my goodness, that sounds so serious."

Frank stared at her, a grave expression on his face. Sarah shifted uncomfortably in her seat. "Yes, yes, Frank. You have my word."

"Good." Frank nodded and relaxed a bit.

"Frank, why don't you tell her about your trip abroad? I found that so fascinating," Ellen offered.

"Oh, you've shown me the pictures," Sarah told him, fidgeting with the crust of her sandwich, although she was losing interest in her food. "But what does that have to do with this?"

"Well, I'll tell you." Frank sat upright in his chair and ran his hand over his broad jaw. "Five years ago, not long after my wife died, I took a trip abroad traveling the world, from India to England, and what I saw expanded me as a person, as a Christian, and it has expanded my notion of God and what spirituality can do for a society." Betty and Ellen beamed up at him. Ellen went on finishing her food as he spoke. "Did you know the Druids and the Hindus built monuments thousands of years old, that still boggle the mind to this day? Some of these cultures . . . it's just riveting. Did you know that many ancient cultures knew the exact locations of the planets, the makeup of their atmospheres, and even their colors, although, as far as we know, they lacked any such technology that would have allowed them access to this information directly?"

"Why, no, I didn't know that. How interesting." Sarah looked around the room. On the walls Betty had hung a few Impressionist images, one of an old farmhouse, nicely framed, and one of a deer leaping through a green wood. On the shelf beside her sat a collection of knickknacks made up of large and small figurines of angels mostly, but on the top shelf, in the center, sat a larger, older-looking statue that was altogether unfamiliar to Sarah.

"Even today, thousands upon thousands of people travel to India each year to learn about their religious and spiritual teachings. It's spreading around the world. And it's spreading because they are flexible. They are more open-minded, you see."

"Have you ever tried yoga?" Ellen interrupted excitedly. Sarah shook her head no. "Tantric yoga. Have you heard of it?"

"Tantric?" Sarah asked. "As in . . . well you mean . . . tantric?"

"It's a practice of very focused exercise that leaves the body feeling quite invigorated," Frank boomed. He took a deep breath as if breathing in clean mountain air and let out a long, healthy hiss, stretching his hands wide as he did so, demonstrating something. "It involves a series of stretches, and other things. I learned about it in India. I gave Ellen a book on it."

Ellen nodded and smiled excitedly. "It's lovely."

"All we're saying," Frank explained, "is that we need to be thinking more in tune with the times. There are so many things other religions have to offer out there, and everyone is mixing ideas and practices, and here we are stuck with a pastor who wants to keep us hunting witches."

Betty raised her hand. "Years ago, when we had a larger congregation, we were able to have more of a presence in the town. You remember. We did the beautification garden in the Main Street square every summer, and I was *proud* to be a member of the Baptist church, with our name up on the sign in the middle of all of those flowers. And we sponsored the cakewalk raffle at the firemen's picnic. But now, since our numbers have been dwindling, well, we just don't have the funding to do things like that anymore, and we don't have access to the community center anymore, either. Now it's the Methodists who have their name on the sign in the Main Street square and have free use of the community center, and now *they* sponsor the cakewalk, *and* the canned food drive."

"The Methodists," Frank grumbled.

"All we want," Betty went on, "is for our church to be respected in the community again. We need that."

"Yes, of course," Sarah nodded, but she wasn't sure what exactly they were getting at, what with all the various and strange turns the conversation had taken.

"Sarah," Frank implored her, "have you ever wondered if perhaps all the religions of all the world are worshiping the same God, but in different forms?"

Sarah sat back in her chair, her mouth open. What he was saying was more than edging on sacrilege, and she thought perhaps Frank's trip to India had made him a bit *too* open-minded. She wondered if he knew the implications of what he was saying.

"Now, hear me out," he went on. "I'm a Baptist. I was born a Baptist and I'll die a Baptist, but that doesn't mean I can't be open, just a little open, to other things as well, does it?"

"I suppose not," Sarah said, stiffening her back and bringing her shoulders up, tensely.

"Instead of driving people away with accusation, wouldn't it be better to have something real and exciting to offer, to bring people in?"

"Well, I suppose so," Sarah said, shaking her head. "But I don't know what you're proposing exactly."

Betty turned and looked her in the eye. "A shift," she said pointedly.

"A shift?"

"We're considering a few options, and we wanted you to weigh in. You are one of the founding members of the church, after all. You should be part of this. Everyone trusts you, as well they should. You've been a pillar of our congregation since it started."

"Sarah, you really have such a kind heart," Ellen added. "You even feed those awful crows when they come begging. It's astonishing." Betty widened her eyes at Ellen. It was a small gesture, but Sarah noticed and found it odd.

"What she means is, you have such generosity, even for the basest creatures," Betty told her kindly.

"Oh, thank you," she said. But it hadn't seemed like a compliment completely.

"What do you know about the Druids?" Ellen chirped.

"I'm sorry?"

"Frank went to Stonehenge," Betty said, smiling and pouring herself some more tea. "It's all very fascinating, and the more I've learned about it, the more I understand that we need to be going in a different direction."

"The more you learn about Stonehenge, you mean? A different direction with the church . . . related to Stonehenge?" Sarah asked perplexedly.

"Sarah," Frank continued, "have you ever studied the history of religious diasporas?"

She sat back and viewed him squarely. "Frank, you sound like

a professor." It occurred to her that maybe she didn't know Frank
that well at all.

"Well, I've been doing a lot of reading, for years now. When my
wife died, and I went abroad for the first time in my life—well, the
first time not counting my time in the army—it changed me. It's
like a whole new chapter began. So, have you ever read about the
world religions and how they've evolved?"

Sarah smiled at him and tried out her tea again. "No, not much.
I suppose I've seen a documentary here and there, but not much
other than that, really. No. I don't know much about it at all."

"Well, it's all fascinating." Frank rested his elbows on the table
on either side of his plate, leaning in. "Everything comes from
something. As you know, Protestants came out of Catholicism,
and us Evangelicals, well, we came directly from Judaism." Sarah
nodded in agreement. "And when you start looking at other religions, the Druids for instance, well, they have ties to many indoc-
trinations of the Christian religion, as well as neo-paganism
dating all the way back to the Iron Age, and maybe beyond."

"I didn't know you were so interested in this type of thing,
Frank," Sarah said.

"Well, like I said, I wasn't, until my trip. I met some very
amazing people, passionate people, in London and Wales. Did
you know that there are still Druids practicing ancient rituals
today, and combining it with all sorts of fascinating theologies?"

"I had no idea." Her eyes were wide though she was trying to
mask her shock. "Druids. Today?" Sarah knew, and she knew
Frank must know as well as she did, Druids were looked at as akin
to a satanic cult, and this was all quite taboo, and it was extremely
odd that he would speak of the Druids so casually, as if they were
just another denomination of Christians, and that the other two

women were reacting as if there were nothing exceptional in what he was saying at all. He was going on about all this quite coolly, and she didn't know how to take it or how to act.

"Yes," Frank continued with his strange history lesson. "They can't say for sure where the first Druids came from. The Celts, the Germans, the Welsh? It seems to have sprung up in different, unconnected parts of the world around the same time, somehow, as if there were something divine or supernatural speaking to these various, unconnected cultures. And after thousands of years, it is still a vibrant religion, because its followers have allowed it to evolve, and have incorporated it into their other beliefs. This is what I'm getting at. As evangelicals, we should be asking, what does the future hold? We should be asking what's *next*? Not reenacting some tired Victorian drama!" The last sentence he spoke loudly, anger and excitement visible in him.

Sarah watched him cautiously. "I've never heard you speak this way," she said softly. "I can't say I totally disagree with you on your last point, but I'm sorry, I just don't understand. What are you proposing we do, exactly?"

"Well," the three looked at each other. Betty took the lead. "At first we thought, last week, when this came out, we thought, maybe it would be best if one of us just came forward with something, anything they've been needing to get off their shoulders. Some confession that would serve to appease Rick and Tracy and we could move on from all this, this . . ."

"This nonsense," Frank interjected.

Betty went on, "Of course, there are still members who stand behind the pastor. It's a conservative little area, and we all live here," she motioned to everyone at the table. "We joined the church because we share the same values. But we do think this may be getting out of hand."

"It reminds me of the eighties, when we got up in arms about Satanists we thought were secretly taking over the town, and it turned out to be nothing more than some teenagers painting graffiti on the bridges. We looked like buffoons. That's what we looked like," Frank said. "I've poured a good amount of money into that church. My family's name is on the bell tower. I'm not going to be run out!"

Betty let out a frustrated sigh. "No one is running you out," she said soothingly.

"Why on earth would anyone want to run you out?" Sarah inquired.

Frank shook his head and gathered himself. "We just aren't sure," Betty told her. "We aren't sure what to do and we wanted you to weigh in. You're the church treasurer after all. You've been here since the beginning and everyone trusts you, Sarah. And well, we are, unfortunately, considering the very real possibility, along with some other members, of asking the pastor to step down."

"Oh dear," Sarah said, shocked.

"Even if," Frank told her, "someone comes forward with a confession of some sort, and this one incident is put to rest, we can't be sure it won't happen again. Obviously, we hope there's another way, but right now, I just don't see any. If the church is going to ever begin to grow and thrive like it did, we can't have this sort of thing continuously going on. These abstract accusations, it puts people off, really, most normal people, it puts them off. It spooks them."

"Well, this is more than I expected. Asking Rick to resign as pastor? I need to take some time to think about all this," Sarah told them. Worry was visible on her face.

"Of *course* you do." Betty reached out and touched her hand. Sarah took a deep breath and looked around the room again, trying to process everything she'd heard. "Asking Rick to step down is a very big decision. Couldn't we maybe just talk to him about the way he's handling his wife?"

"We could," Ellen said. "*You* could. He trusts you."

"Oh?" Sarah let out a heavy sigh.

"He's just gotten so paranoid," Ellen continued. "He doesn't even want Betty and me to have keys to the basement anymore."

"The basement?" Sarah asked. Betty shook her head no at Ellen. But Ellen didn't notice, or at least pretended not to.

"You know Betty and I clean the church on alternating Saturdays, and we have the keys to the church, as do you, of course, you're the treasurer. You *do* also have keys to the basement, don't you, Sarah?"

"Well, yes. I haven't been down there in years, but, yes, I do. I have the master key. All the remaining founders do." She was becoming very confused.

"Oh, terrific!" Ellen said. "That's terrific. That's what we thought." Sarah tilted her head. "Rick is getting odd, is all. It's more than just Tracy," Ellen told her.

"He's closed-minded is what it is," Frank said sternly.

"He's asked us to turn in our basement keys," Betty snapped. "And the whole thing is just too weird for words." She shot an angry look in Ellen's direction. "I don't even know why we're talking about this, really. This isn't relevant."

"Well, I happen to think it is," Ellen snapped back. "It shows his mind-set."

"Why on earth," Sarah asked, "would he give two whips about the basement?"

"The church is consecrated ground. It was built there on the old cemetery, and the tombs in the back are precious relics."

"What?" Sarah had gotten completely lost. Why Frank was bringing this up, she couldn't understand. The church was indeed built on a cemetery with family tombs dating back to the late 1600s. Years before they broke ground, another church had been there, housed in a building that was not much more than a barn. The ground was a historic site, but what this had to do with anything, she had no idea. And what did the cemetery in the backyard have to do with the basement?

"You've barely touched your food," Betty told her. "Is everything all right?"

"Oh, I think I'm finished with this. Thank you," Sarah told her.

"How about I cut some of that lemon cake you brought and get us some dessert?"

"That sounds just fine," Sarah told her, her voice shrill and pinched.

"I'll help you," Ellen said, rising and clearing the plates from the table with Betty. The two women disappeared into the kitchen, and Sarah could hear them murmuring in the other room.

She sat at the table alone with Frank. The two stared at one another, Sarah keeping up a tense, disingenuous smile. Frank finally broke the silence. "I'm sorry, I know this is a lot for you to take in. We just, well, I in particular, had a feeling about you, that you would be open to hearing our ideas and concerns."

"And I am. And I also share some of your concerns," she assured him.

"Yes, well," Frank placed an elbow on the table and leaned toward her, "even more than that, I've always thought you were someone very special. You seem like an open-minded person."

Sarah shifted in her seat. She didn't quite know what to make of the way he was talking to her. She didn't want to like it, but some part of her that she couldn't deny did like it very much. She blushed and looked down at her plate. "Thank you, Frank. You flatter me."

He laid his palm on the table near her. "I can be open with you, can't I, Sarah?" She looked him in the eye. He was gazing quite intently at her, with a trace of a soft and, she couldn't help but think, flirtatious smile lighting his lips.

"Of course, Frank. Of course."

"Right. I'm just going to tell you, we've been meeting in the basement on Saturday nights, having a sort of prayer gathering in the fashion that many of us would like to see the church becoming more open to, and we'd like you to join us."

Her mouth clamped shut and her skin tingled. What was he talking about? Was this really happening? He couldn't be implying what she thought he was implying. "You've been having prayer meetings at the church . . . in the basement? Why didn't you announce it to the entire congregation?"

"No," he whispered and shook his head. "Not everyone can know." He paused and sat back up straight, folding his napkin in his lap. "Rick and Tracy can never know."

"What?" she asked again, astonished. The sound of Betty and Ellen's footsteps prompted Frank to place his finger to his lips and pantomime a "shhh."

"Here it is. What a lovely dessert!" Betty proclaimed, as she and Ellen placed the plates of lemon cake in front of Sarah and Frank and resumed their seats. "Dig in." The other three scooped up the yellow cake with their forks, white frosting mushing between the prongs. Sarah sat motionless, a stunned expression on her face, processing what Frank had just said to her. She was still staring directly at him, though he was no longer paying her any attention and had taken to vigorously enjoying his desert. She didn't know how to proceed. She leaned farther back in the chair and took an account of the three of them, going on as if everything were normal.

She shook her head and looked around the room again, and once more noticing the strange object on the shelf, she turned to get a better look at it.

It was made of a greenish stone. It was a male figure that could have been, she thought, an African tribesman of some sort with a small round head, and his mouth wide open, sitting cross-legged, holding up what appeared to be a rope in one hand, and from his head was growing what she thought looked like deer antlers, but it was hard to make anything out for sure from where she was sitting. "What is that thing?" she let out, sounding more obviously disturbed than she would have liked. The three others stopped eating, Ellen in mid-bite, and regarded her with worry.

"That's nothing," Betty said, waving her hand. "Just a little thing I picked up."

"Betty," Frank put down his fork and stood, "it's fine. Let's tell her about it."

Betty sighed and lifted her shoulders. "Well, all right, it *is* odd. But, well, it's an artifact, really, an antique."

"It's mine." Frank lifted it from the shelf and displayed it for Sarah.

"It's yours? Why is it here then?" Sarah asked shrilly, her voice trembling.

"Frank . . . umm, he loaned it to me," Betty said.

"*Loaned* it to you? For what?"

"Just so I can . . ." she was at a loss for words and becoming visibly frustrated although trying to keep a pleasant look on her face in spite of everything, "so I can enjoy it, until he needs it again."

"*Needs* it again?" Sarah snapped. "What would he *need* it for?"

"Why are you so upset?" Ellen asked.

"It's hideous," Sarah said, shaking her head no.

"Maybe we should take a break. Go out back on the porch and get some fresh air," Betty tried. "We've given Sarah so much to think about. It's been such an emotional day."

"Nonsense," Frank said, walking toward Sarah and setting the statue down on the table in front of her. "This is nothing to be upset about. Take a look. It's just an antique. It's a stone figure is all. You see?"

"What on earth is it supposed to be?" Sarah asked, leaning in to get a closer look.

"This is Cernunnos, or the Horned God, who was, and is still, worshiped by the Druids, and sacred to a number of religious people all over the world." Sarah leaned back, away from the thing. "He's nothing to fear. He's a hunter, a forest creature, a man—"

"Does it have an *erection*?" The words just came out of her thoughtlessly, in a harsh, angry whisper. Betty's eyes were wide with worry. Ellen sat across from her covering her hands with her mouth as if she were a child being caught at something.

"Yes, Sarah, he does have an erection," Frank told her matter-of-factly. "In many heathen cultures, an erection is nothing to be ashamed of. Not everyone views sex in such a strict light as we do here. For some, it's a simple, pleasant function of the human body, and for some even, an activity enjoyed together, amongst many . . . in a group." He raised an eyebrow at her. "What do you think of that?"

"Those heathens," Betty said shrilly, "what will they think of next? Of course, they don't know any better."

"My god, Betty!" Sarah said, locking eyes with her friend.

Betty finally stopped smiling and her expression revealed despair. She placed her hand over Sarah's and grasped it tightly. "Sarah, please," she whispered. "I just thought you would—"

"Thought I would what?"

"Understand!" Betty pleaded. Ellen shoved her chair back and left the room. Sarah didn't look away from Betty.

"Please don't be like this. It's nothing bad."

Sarah felt pity for her friend and saw the desperation in her eyes. She couldn't help thinking that just an hour before, she herself feared being persecuted, even ostracized, for her own transgression. But this was different, wasn't it? They knew what they were doing. What *were* they doing? A part of her wanted to know more, while she tried to tell herself she'd heard all she needed, much more than enough.

She was deeply relieved to know that the darkness in the church did not reside with her, after all. She never would have thought it was so insidious and specific a secret as what she'd discovered.

"It's nothing bad?" she hissed at Betty. "Just some, what? Orgies in the church basement? Is that it? My god! And this thing." She pushed the statue away from her and covered her face with her hands.

"You're being *such a prude*!" Betty squealed, slapping the table with the palm of her hand, and biting her lip.

"Ladies, ladies," Frank said soothingly. He stepped up closer behind Sarah, who was hunched over, still covering her face with her hands, and began massaging her shoulders. "It's been a difficult conversation. We're all worked up." Sarah wanted to pull away from his touch but his strong hands on her neck and shoulders sent a sensation through her body, and she felt like she was melting, and though she tried resisting, she gave into his touch, and even relaxed. "Let's take a deep breath," Frank went on. She felt dizzy, overcome, and her mind was absolutely racing. She kept beginning to cry, then stopping and nearly hyperventilating. Frank breathed in deeply, and exhaled slowly. Her head was awash with contradictory emotion. "Sarah, everything is fine, there's nothing to be upset about. You've known us almost all your life. You don't think we're bad people, do you?"

"I don't know. I don't know what to think."

"Come now," Frank said, pulling her back so that her head rested against his torso. She placed a hand over his where it rested on her shoulder. "How could you do this?" she murmured.

"I think we all just need to calm down and clear our heads. Betty's right." He slid his thumbs up and then down Sarah's shoulders. Sarah sighed, despite herself. She was appalled, but at the same time, though she hated to admit it, she was excited. She wanted to get up and run away, but she also, in spite of herself, wanted to stay and find out what exactly they wanted with her. Why had they decided to let her in? Was it simply because they wanted her keys to the basement, or was it something else, something they'd seen in her, like Frank had said, something exceptional and strange about her, that she also knew, and often feared she possessed, some restlessness that was a lust and more than that, a deep need for more, more of anything from life?

"I feel dizzy," she said. "I feel sick. I feel just sick to my stomach."

Frank shook her gently. "Come on. Let's all go out on the porch and take in some fresh air. That'll help. How does that sound?"

Sarah nodded, feeling overcome. "Fresh air. Oh yes, that could be good," she agreed. "Let's all go out on the porch and get some fresh air."

THINGS TO DO WHEN YOU'RE GOTH IN THE COUNTRY

W hen I was sixteen, I used to sit under the bell tower with my friends and smoke. Smoking was something to do. The little courtyard under the bell tower was like nothing else in the town. It looked European to us. A pointless enclave situated between three buildings with iron benches and a small stone fountain; that's all it was. Completely impractical and unlike anything else. There was never anyone there. We were the only ones in town who were in any way interested in that courtyard. It was a hip pocket where the universe opened up in the middle of that ugly rural town and allowed things to seem cosmopolitan for one hundred and fifty square feet. All we did there was smoke because no one could see us back there and we were too young to legally smoke cigarettes. Cigarettes tasted better there. That taste they have when you don't smoke often and it's new, that's what it was. The smell of Marlboros and Camels are two very different things, but both are savory when smoking is new to you, and taste like a fresh croissant in Paris your first day in town. That's how cigarettes tasted to me there under the bell tower when I was sixteen.

One time, I'd been smoking too much for a few days, and cigarettes didn't taste new anymore, they just tasted burning and sick. I was sitting on the ledge of the fountain under the bell tower, the fancy cobblestone under my boots, the thick foliage behind the fountain casting shade and a hot August sun at three o'clock. Sweat dripped down my nose. I pulled out a cigarette. My friends stood around preparing to do something: smoke. I said, "It's too hot to smoke." They all laughed and repeated what I'd said, "Too hot to smoke." I felt very cool. I knew in that moment that, whatever happened, I was going to be all right, we all were, because we could find a way to be hip, even there in the middle of nowhere: Bible Belt, cow country, abandoned train-town. I lit a cigarette and forced it down, making myself sick. The bell tower started gonging. We all looked up into the sunlight reflecting off the windows of the bell tower.

There's a girl I like to tell things to. She doesn't like to be called a woman, even though she is. I like to tell her these pointless things because they are prizes the trick claw of my brain catches and drops into her lap, worthless as purple stuffed elephants but celebrated in the moment because they got hooked against the odds and extracted. She gives me these things too. We keep passing quarters, piling up pretty plastic toys that look so different hanging in a difficult claw than they did on the worthless heap of memory.

She looks like trash to me, and I like it. I've spent years polishing it away, worrying that people could see right through my bag. My cow-shaped under-chin when I tilt my head might be a tell. I check skin tone for smoothness and pockmarks. My stomach is a dead giveaway. But I've been assured none of these things are trash markers to anyone other than me. I've been assured it's not visible to the outside world. Then I look at her, and it's so obvious. The trash signs are everywhere, even through her queerness. Queerness un-trashes people a little, or it can. (Sometimes it goes in the opposite direction, though.) Still, I can see what she would be without the good sex, weird haircut, and interesting clothes, clear as a dump truck at dawn. And I know also, when I look at her, for all my polishing, my face must be the same sort of obviousness and there was never anything I could have done about it. Trash gets into the body and forms it, molds speech and jawlines. It scars the skin with acne kisses from too many greasy-fry dinners. Just overhearing things like Guns N' Roses and Bon Jovi rots the teeth and yellows the eyes.

It's something about things. Things like things that hurt. Like whipped cream. $2.49. Something I did that became a thing for a moment. A thing for a moment because it abstracted everything and right then I wanted nothing to do with anything anymore that wasn't abstract and indecipherable; that wasn't a vague term.

Whippets turn the world into vague terms. My cousin and I had the same feeling about these days. So we went to the store at dusk all year and purchased cans of generic whipped cream, the aerosol kind. Then we went to the park. Then the sun would be setting. Then we laid down our sixteen-year-old trashy girl bodies on the merry-go-round. Then we pushed with our feet so that we were spinning. Then we tilted the jagged plastic nozzles of the whipped cream aerosol canisters to our lips. You don't shake the bottle. You don't want any cream to come out. Just the gas. We pushed the nozzle sideways and sucked. Inhaled. The nozzles have jagged tips for decorating. If you are dressing an ice cream sundae, the jagged edge makes the whipped cream wavy. It makes patterns, like stars. The gas creamed us. The gas cut stars out of our minds. Made us soft edges left over. The park was always blue-gray and empty just after dusk, and newly cool, and we spun, and everything hummed and became a vague terminology of dusk-glowing trees, cement, and swing sets. Our minds were creamy stars poking through the dusk, waving us goodbye.

It's something about things that hurt, how they stay and shape the body. Things that you seek pleasure in when you're trashy. It makes you tell stories like this. Like we were basically huffing glue, but it seemed sweet because it smelled like whipped cream. It makes vague terminology very appealing.

I looked different than my cousin while we were tripping from fumes on the merry-go-round. I looked better. Which meant I was. I liked to draw upside-down crosses below my eyes, like two sacrilegious tears ending above my cheeks. I wanted to draw Jesus there on them, a black silhouette of him hanging upside down. I drew upside-down crosses under my eyes and purchased a silver grill cut with upside-down crucifixes I wore on my three upper front teeth, and went around the country roads on my mountain bike when I was fifteen. I liked to go stand in the middle of cornfields in the autumn in a black bowler and trench coat and pretend I'd painted the sky, grinning my upside-down silver Jesus grill toward the pink sunset.

I was like a cat that way: staring at skylines, staring at ghosts. We liked to go to the haunted bridge in the next town over. Three towns away there was a haunted ditch, and in the country roads between Nashville and Hoyleton, Illinois, there was a haunted bump. You had to know exactly where that haunted bump was or you would never find it since it was on an unmarked black tar road with only trees on one side and a cornfield on the other, repeating for miles, and no markers. The knowledge of where that bump was got passed down to you from other people, and then you had to really memorize it before you showed anyone else, be taken there a few times, or else you'd end up at the wrong bump in the road late at night and try to do that haunted thing that we did at that bump, and it wouldn't work, because you weren't paying enough attention and parked your car on some other, ordinary, everyday, non-haunted bump in that road. And then nothing would happen. Then you would just be some kids sitting in a car near a bump in the road waiting in vain to be haunted.

I experienced the bump haunting three times. I went looking for it, seeking out a fourth haunted bump experience, but by myself for once, and instead I saw a UFO that I had to drive very fast to get away from, and I never went back to that haunted bump again.

The haunted bump haunting was a very mechanical kind of haunting. If you situated yourself just right, it would happen every time like ghostly clockwork. It wasn't as finicky as my haunted bridge. The ghost of the haunted bridge would only come out very sporadically, and even when she did, it was debatable what had actually happened. This bump's manner of haunting was not debatable.

The thing you had to do was park your car three yards past

the bump and facing east. This situates your car sloping down a not very steep hill, front pointing downhill with the bump uphill behind you. It's very important that you understand exactly what I am saying about the situating of the car, or else it won't be obvious why what is about to happen when you do this is so scary.

Okay. So now you're sitting there. You're sloping downhill. Put the car in neutral. Turn it off. Leave it on. Either way. I usually turned it off so I could hear the cicadas for added effect. When the car is off and in neutral, it is natural that the car will roll forward, downhill. At first, it doesn't move at all. For several minutes, it just sits there. But then, it starts rolling, *backward, uphill*, gaining speed as it goes, faster and faster, backward, uphill, in the middle of the dark woods, until it gets over that bump, all the way over by a few yards, and then the car slides off to the side of the road into the dirt shoulder. Then it stops. Then you've experienced the haunted bump.

What's actually happening there is, a school bus crashed there in the sixties. Right there past that bump, and twenty kids died. The bus stalled in the middle of the road there and a drunk driver of a pickup truck crashed into it. The ghosts of those kids want to reverse their death over and over. Ghosts are very associative. So if you go there with any vehicle and stop where they crashed, which happens to be by that bump which is the only marker, they will come and push you back, then leave your car off to the side on the dirt shoulder, out of harm's way.

I wonder how anyone found out about that haunted bump in the first place. It must have taken a lot of sitting around. There's a lot of free time in the country.

My friends once tested the ghost children theory and went to the bump with bags of flour. They covered the car in flour and tossed it on the road there by that bump. Then they situated the car correctly for the haunting and sat in the car and waited. It rolled backward, uphill and all. The haunting worked as it did every time. Then they got out of the car and took out their flashlights, and they found children's handprints in the flour that covered the car. About twenty pairs of them, and footprints in the flour on the road as well. Then they all pissed their pants.

I've only pissed my pants three times in my entire life, and always when I was sleeping. Once when I was just out of diapers. Once when I was thirteen and had pneumonia with a fever of 104. And once when I was seventeen. It was just a very bad dream. But I'd been cutting myself all day the day before I went to sleep in that nightmare. (Cutting is also something to do, like smoking.) And then, in the summers especially, maintenance of cutting adds some other activities. Self-mutilation in the summer requires styling the legs of black panty hose to be worn like chic long-gloves over the blood-caked scabs. This way you can still wear T-shirts and be cool in the midwestern humidity.

There is nothing like pissing yourself from a nightmare, with scabs on your arms. Waking up, a year away from legal adulthood, to wet yellow sheets in the wavering sunlight below dust-drenched windows will make you understand your own fragility in a way only akin to suddenly realizing you are elderly. It's a gray happening.

Nearly, but not quite, as shocking as surprise exorcisms. If you are going to be Goth in the country and really go for it, I would highly recommend a nonconsensual, surprise Southern Baptist exorcism. There's just nothing else that can compete. That moment when your minister lays hands on you, and the faces of the congregation, people you thought you knew well, turn, doll-eyed and pitying, to begin praying some unknown demon out of you, their lips mouthing out whisperings of the same prayer in unison: that really is the pinnacle.

It's going to take a lot to cause this occurrence. You will have to commit yourself to a very particular type of disturbance in order to get an entire congregation of Southern Baptists to conspire with God against your soul. You don't have to do exactly what I did, but I'll share my experience as a template that can be reworked and altered, specifically tailored for your own personal CG (country Goth) experience.

Always begin with the Bible. I took advantage of my church duties. Wednesday night Bible study was a rotation. There were twelve regular members, myself included. Mine was an enforced attendance. Each week, a different Bible study member selected the text to be read and studied. Every twelfth week was my week to select the text, read it aloud to the congregation, and then sit through an hour-long discussion. For this, I utilized Halloween paint. It is very important to approach all unpleasant tasks in life as a performance art piece, especially if you are a teenager. On Wednesday nights, I dressed like I was going to kill a Marilyn Manson concert. I approached the pulpit with my big red Bible, held my hands out like an offering, and spread the Bible open, the thick, soft pages resting splayed and flowing out like a woman's thick parted thighs. My scabs healing underneath the hacked-up panty hose I wore on my arms. Chains rattling from my hips, and fucked-up Barbie doll-head necklaces hanging around my neck; Vietnam ear tokens honoring the violence of girlishness. There I stood before the congregation in the small steepled white church, under the empty cross, exposed rafters echoing barnyards, my eyes painted thick with black curlicues swirling up from my lids to around my temples, and upside-down black crosses resting like tears above my cheeks. My white powdered cheeks, sparkling fake-blood-red lips, and hot-pink dreadlocks sticking out from beneath a black bowler.

And I read them their Bible. I read the congregation their sacred text, dressed that way on their pulpit. I spoke in a booming, deep-throated voice that, at moments, devolved into a growl, echoing through their sanctuary like it was a black magic road show we were doing. I read them their Ezekiel. I read them their sacred book and I made it mine. I made their reverence my blasphemy, my sacrilege.

It was the word of the Lord I was reading, and more importantly, it was the word of *their* Lord saying through my horrible mouth, *"And I will lay the dead carcasses of the children before their idols; and I will scatter your bones round about your altars."* And saying, *"I will drench the land with your flowing blood all the way to the mountains, and the ravines will be filled with your flesh."* And saying, *"And they shall know that I am the LORD, and that I have not said in vain that I would do this evil."*

It was like a song I was singing to them, like low screamcore, like they'd never heard the words so crisp and clear before. *And the earth will become flesh and the birds will peck at the flesh until the rivers are rivers of blood, for I am the Lord your God,* sort of thing. It was my best performance piece ever. It was the best because it was happening in real time, in real space, on holy ground, making righteous people question and gawk and quake a little. I would go so far as to say there was some quaking. And there was a woman named Betty there. That made it really terrific.

It's things like this you will have to do to reach the pinnacle point (the pinnacle point being nonconsensual exorcism by people you have known all your life). Carving pentacles into your forehead with razor blades is always an option as well and requires less setup and performative skill. I prefer pentacles to pentagrams, as I find pentagrams to be a bit of an overkill, and rather silly as Satanism is so blasé and reactionary an endeavor. I also highly recommend being a homosexual. Rural Goth trash just reads better homo. If you are not already a homosexual, you can easily become one. I became one as young as the age of five, so it will be all the easier to do in adolescence at a time when most have a more developed aesthetic understanding of the libido.

Oh there are so many things to do.

You can harass military recruiters who set up tables in your school's lunchroom by brandishing neon feather boas and dancing around them singing Adam Ant's "You're Just Too Physical" as reworked by Trent Reznor, for instance. You will definitely want to spend a lot of time in the old part of the cemetery, just hanging out, then tell people about it. If you are very ambitious, write some poems there. I always did. Try some necromancy just for kicks, if you are wanting to be a true professional. Don't tell anyone about that. Some things we must keep to ourselves.

When I was very young, I had a voice in a well that I kept all to myself. As commanded by the voice in the well, our conversations were kept secret, and that was for the best, in retrospect, I am sure. The voice in the well was gray as the stone that housed it. It was a very grounded male voice of wisdom that told me many important things. It began telling me things when I was five years old; then when I was eight, my family cemented the well and it was covered then and I couldn't hear the voice anymore. But when I could it told me many important things. It told me to never grow up. It told me to always smell the grass. It told me the wind would guide and protect me and loved me unconditionally because I was exceptionally beautiful to the wind in my area. It told me where to find dead things.

I found many dead things guided by the voice in the well. One dead cow, legs pointing straight up toward the afternoon sky and stiff like Viagra meat. I found one dead dog gutted in the woods by a homeless man who'd been living there all summer. It was a golden retriever mix of something, and its belly was sliced open, full of maggots and flies so thick it looked like the thick love I had for the friend I found it with, and I would only have ever wanted to find something so perfectly fucked up with someone I loved as much as I loved that blond girl. The Air Force stole her perfect heart years later.

I found a nest of rabbits drowned in puddles; drowned by the bare hands of my six-year-old cousin who had spent the previous night glassy-eyed and babbling prophecies about stillborn kittens. So many dead birds fallen, innumerable deer, one dead squirrel I had known, and many dead classmates at funerals I attended during the summers when teenagers liked to have deadly wrecks or drown in lakes and flooded ponds. I found death in the eyes of friends who began enlisting in the military so they didn't have to become farmers and break the legs of chickens with hormones. It was a deep well of death in their eyes and there were voices there too, but they were not my voice.

My voice in the well was gray and kind. My voice in the well was also probably dead. The voice in my well told me the most important thing and the most difficult thing. It told me empathy. Repeatedly. It told me, "Empathy. Child. Be a child. Be an empathetic child. Always. All we kill is ourselves." It told me, "All we love is ourselves." It told me, "All. We. Kill. Is. Our. Selves."

The black helicopter's sonic booms are classified information and officially do not exist, but when they happened, everyone would come down off their porches and stand looking up. They would say, "Air Force base," and point west. When the swarms of black helicopters would pass over us in moments of bad consciousness I would remember the voice in the well saying, "Empathy. Child. All we kill is ourselves." I would look to the farmers saying, "Air Force," pointing their calloused fingers west and feel the wars which are endless and meant to be endless ripping open my guts with their flapping blades and I would know I was dead too. And I would know for a moment that it wasn't only me painting my eyes so black and my skin so pale. It wasn't something autonomous inside me making me need to look so dead. Dead as the kids dropping hands like bricks, and the carcasses of children God promised to spread around vain altars. Dead as the elite Republican Guard. Dead as Iraqi insurgents and people just trying to drive their cars home to dinner on the only road home that is awfully near a pipeline. Dead as oil and sand. Dead as the conscientiousness of this country that grew me up in vast cornfields jabbering with upside-down silver Jesus teeth at broken-egg-gone-bad sunsets that spill and spill and spill, as if there's nothing to lose, ever. You could find me wagging my crotch and scars at the warplanes that do not exist deafeningly in vast cornfields at sunset. Trench. Coat. Dread. Locks. Bowler.

Do not take the sky for granted. It falls all the time somewhere. And now there are kids wagging there at drones, wagging their fucked-up trash at no one, at video screens below the cracking sky spilling out orange paths for strange jets and helicopters. So many insects. Mosquitoes and fruit flies. If you want to do it right, let them suck on you. Don't smack anything painful away. The country itches. It eats you and burns. Always be prepared for the apocalypse. Or rather, be willing to see the apocalypse that is happening around you. Even when it is silent as glass and you can see nothing for miles except the miles stretching out to more miles. Know that it is out there, bred by where you are and so always present to you exploding the silence in silence.

Run through the fields in boots or barefooted in pressed suits and never comb your hair for any reason unless it is to be a dandy. Run through the fields to the woods and collect all the dead things. Curse all manifestations of monotheistic nation God. Masturbate to ghosts by the haunted creek and let your cumming flow long as time that stretches out and lasts so long in this place where people build things like scarecrows and pits and mud is a verb. Hang dolls in trees and let them blow in the wind. Return daily to watch their decay. Cut blood out of yourself and feed it in droplets to the creek like little boats the creek is always hungry for. Let the boats go to be devoured at the mouth or the bend. Let the boats go on like dead crows on the water of endless time that will rot to fertilize a more elaborate nothing of this land of dust and imbecilic violence concealed below the scent of earth, fresh cut wheat, and bleach for their fresh starched linens that glow on clotheslines at twilight like spectral flags. This is where you belong. There is much to be done.

Brooklyn-based writer CHAVISA WOODS is the author of *The Albino Album* (Seven Stories Press, 2013) and *Love Does Not Make Me Gentle or Kind* (Fly by Night Press, 2009). Woods was the recipient of the 2014 Cobalt Prize for fiction and was a finalist in 2009 and 2014 for the Lambda Literary Award for fiction. She has appeared as a featured author at the Whitney Museum of American Art, City Lights Bookstore, Seattle Town Hall, the Brecht Forum, the Cervantes Institute, and the St. Mark's Poetry Project.